To Gideon Joel Parfitt
From   Grandma Jamie
with   love
Happy 4th Birthday!

Four Days With Aunt Joanne

Four Days With Aunt Joanne

Writer: Mary Hursh

Artist: Jessica Kauenhofen

Rod and Staff Publishers, Inc.
P. O. Box 3, Hwy. 172
Crockett, Kentucky 41413
Telephone (606) 522-4348

Copyright 2004
Rod and Staff Publishers, Inc.
Crockett, Kentucky 41413

Printed in U.S.A

ISBN 0-7399-2309-9
Catalog no. 2264

2   3   4   5   6   —   15   14   13   12   11   10   09   08   07   06

To
all my dear
little friends,
through whom God
has richly blessed my life.

Contents

1.

Four Days With Aunt Joanne

A Trip for Father and Mother

"I like my little kitty," Valerie said, gently pet-ting the calico kitten in her arms. "What did Mother say I could name her? I forget."

"Mother said *Callie* would be a good name for her because she is a calico cat," Rhonda answered. She stroked her own kitten's white fur. "I'm going to call mine Powder Puff."

"That's a funny name," laughed Clarence. "But I like it anyway. I don't mind if there are only two baby kittens. Shep is a good friend for me." The big dog heard his name and came over to nuzzle Clarence's shoulder.

"Children," Mother called from the porch, "come inside, please."

Rhonda and Valerie put the kittens back in their nest in the corner of the garage. Then the three children went running to Mother. "Is it bedtime already?" Rhonda asked.

"Not yet," Mother answered. "But Father and I have something we want to talk to you about."

The children followed Mother into the house. Father was sitting on the living room sofa holding little Amy. Rhonda and Clarence sat down, one on each side of Father. Mother sat in the big overstuffed chair, and Valerie squeezed in beside her. "What do you want to talk to us about, Father?" Clarence asked, looking up at Father.

"Do you children remember Glen Byler?" Father asked. "He was here last summer with his mother and father to visit us."

"Is he the boy who is sick like Clarence?" Rhonda asked.

Clarence looked down at his shoes. "I'm not sick," he objected.

"Well, if you didn't take your pills every day, you would be sick," Rhonda said. "And you have to go to the doctor sometimes for tests."

"Let's not argue, children," Father said. "Yes,

Glen had the same sickness that Clarence has. Now Glen's father called and told us that Glen died this morning."

Rhonda's eyes got big. "He died? Why did he die, Father?"

"The other children in his family had bad colds," Father explained. "Glen became very sick, and his body was not strong enough to fight off the germs. They took him to the hospital last night, but he died this morning."

"Couldn't the doctors help him?" Clarence asked.

"No, this time they couldn't," Father answered. "Doctors can do many things for us. But when someone is very, very sick, even doctors cannot always help. This time it was God's will to heal Glen by taking him home to heaven.

"Now," Father continued, "Mother and I would like to go to the funeral. Glen's family lives in Missouri, so it will take us a whole day to drive there."

"Will we go too?" Valerie asked.

"No. We decided that you children will stay with Aunt Joanne," Father answered. Aunt Joanne was Father's oldest sister, and she was not married. She lived in a house close to Grandpa's.

"Oh, goody! I like to stay with Aunt Joanne!" Rhonda exclaimed. "She plays with us."

"This time you will be there for four days," Father said. "I am sure you will enjoy it. But you must remember that Aunt Joanne cannot play with you all the time. She will have work to do too."

"Will we sleep there?" Valerie asked.

"Yes, you will sleep there three nights," Mother said.

"I don't want to sleep there," Valerie said. "I want my own bed."

"Aunt Joanne will probably let you sleep with Rhonda," Mother said, putting her arm comfortingly around Valerie. "Then it will seem almost like your own bed."

"When will we go?" Rhonda asked.

"The day after tomorrow," Father answered. "Tomorrow Mother will pack our clothes and things. Then on Friday morning we will get up early and take you to Aunt Joanne's house before we start on our trip."

"When will you come home?" the children asked.

"We should get home soon after supper on Monday evening, Lord willing," Father explained.

"That seems like a long time," Clarence said slowly.

"I think you will enjoy staying at Aunt Joanne's house," Mother said kindly. "But I know that I will be glad to see my children again after four days."

"Now you children may go out and play for a little while yet before bedtime," Father said.

The children scampered out the door. Rhonda and Valerie ran around the house to play in the sandbox, but Clarence did not feel like playing. He sat on the porch steps, looking very sober.

A few minutes later Mother came outside. "Why, Clarence, what is the matter?" she asked, looking at his sober face. She sat down beside him and put her arm around his shoulder. "Are you thinking about Glen?"

Clarence nodded. "Mother, will I die too?"

Mother was quiet for a moment. "Clarence," she began, "none of us know how long God wants us to live here on the earth. People may live to be very old, like your great-grandfather Clark. And others die when they are children, like Glen. God has a plan for all of our lives. Even healthy people can die. They might have an accident, or they might get sick very suddenly.

"We should not worry about dying, Clarence," Mother went on. "The Bible says, 'Precious in the sight of the LORD is the death of his saints.' When Christians die, they go to heaven to live with God always. God is happy when they come to live with Him. When children die, they go to live with Jesus too. In heaven they will never be sick or sad, and they will never be tempted to do wrong things."

Mother smiled at Clarence. "Maybe God will choose to take you to heaven when you are still a little boy, like He did Glen. But you do not need to be afraid, because then you can go to heaven and be with Jesus. And someday we hope that our whole family can be together in heaven."

Clarence smiled. "I won't be afraid anymore," he said. "Jesus is my friend, and if I die, I can see Him in heaven!"

"That is right," Mother agreed with a smile. "And now it's bedtime. You may call the girls."

2.

Four Days With Aunt Joanne

Rhonda Is a Helper

"Rhonda." Mother shook her gently on Friday morning. "It's time to get up."

Rhonda rolled over sleepily. "Why so early?" she mumbled. "It's still dark outside."

"This is the day you go to Aunt Joanne's house," Mother reminded her.

Rhonda was wide awake now. She jumped out of bed. It did not take her long to put on the clothes that Mother had put on the chair for her. Mother woke Valerie and helped her get dressed. Then they all went downstairs.

Clarence was already in the kitchen. He was sitting on a chair, tying his shoes. "I beat you," he announced, grinning at Rhonda. Rhonda wrinkled her nose at him.

"You children may go out to the car," Father said as he came in for more suitcases.

"Won't we eat any breakfast?" Clarence asked.

"You will eat at Aunt Joanne's house," Father explained. "It's still two hours before the time we usually eat breakfast."

Mother came out of the bedroom carrying Amy, who was still sound asleep. "Are we all ready?" she asked.

"I think so," Father answered, looking around the kitchen.

Mother and the children followed Father outside. Father set down the suitcases to lock the door. Then they all went to the car.

"Here we go!" Rhonda chanted as Father backed the car out the lane. "Here we go to Aunt Joanne's house!"

"You children must remember to be good for Aunt Joanne," Father reminded them as he drove in Aunt Joanne's driveway. "Mother and I want you to obey Aunt Joanne just like you obey us at home. Rhonda and Clarence, you remember to be good helpers. The little ones might get a bit homesick sometimes, and maybe you can help Aunt Joanne to keep them happy."

"We'll try," Clarence promised, and Rhonda nodded her head.

When the car stopped, the three older children tumbled out and ran toward the house. Aunt Joanne met them at the door with a smile on her face. "Come in! Come in!" she welcomed.

"We're going to have fun at your house," Valerie said, smiling up at Aunt Joanne.

"I hope you will," Aunt Joanne replied, giving Valerie a hug. "I will enjoy having you here too."

Mother put Amy to bed; then she and Aunt Joanne talked for a few minutes.

"Okay, I guess it's time to leave," Father said, looking at his watch. "Be good, children. Lord willing, we will call when we get to Missouri."

Rhonda, Clarence, and Valerie watched from the kitchen window as Father and Mother walked to the car. They waved as Father backed the car out the driveway, and Father and Mother waved back. Then the car drove down the road and out of sight.

A tear rolled down Valerie's cheek. Aunt

Joanne noticed it, and she said brightly, "Shall we read some stories?"

"Yes, read!" Valerie's face brightened. "May I choose a story?"

"Yes, you may," Aunt Joanne answered.

Valerie found the book *Molly Helps Mother.* "This one," she said, climbing onto Aunt Joanne's lap.

Aunt Joanne read that book. Then she read several other stories. "Now shall we eat some breakfast?" she said after a while. "How would you like scrambled eggs and toast?"

"Yum, yum," said Rhonda and Clarence.

They were just finishing breakfast when they heard a loud wa-a-a from the bedroom.

"Amy is awake," Aunt Joanne said. She hurried to the bedroom.

Aunt Joanne dressed Amy and changed her diaper. Amy kept on crying all the while. "Ma-ma-ma!" she cried.

"Here, would you like some breakfast?" Aunt Joanne asked. She put a bite of egg on a spoon and offered it to Amy. But Amy turned her head away.

"Shall I hold her?" Rhonda asked. "Father said that Clarence and I should help you keep the little ones happy if they get homesick."

"Yes, maybe that would help," Aunt Joanne said. "She knows you better because you are one of her family."

Rhonda sat down in Aunt Joanne's big chair, and Aunt Joanne put Amy in her lap. Amy laid her head down on Rhonda's shoulder. She sniffled for a while, but finally she got quiet.

"Shall we look at a book, Amy?" Rhonda asked.

"Book, book," Amy said, and a smile chased her tears away.

"May I sit beside you, Rhonda?" Valerie asked.

"Sure." Rhonda slid over to make room for her little sister. Together they looked at the pictures in one of Aunt Joanne's books. It was a story of a little boy who visited his grandpa's farm.

After a while Amy slid off Rhonda's lap and toddled over to the toy box. She found a doll and sat on the floor, trying to take its cap off.

Aunt Joanne watched her with a smile. Then she looked at Rhonda. "Amy didn't eat any breakfast. But I'm afraid if I try to feed her, she will cry again. Would you like to give her some crackers?"

"Yes, I will," Rhonda answered. "She likes crackers."

Aunt Joanne went to the cupboard and got out the cracker box. She handed two crackers to Rhonda. Rhonda took them over to Amy. "Here, Amy, are you hungry?" she asked.

Amy reached eagerly for a cracker. She stuffed it into her mouth and reached for the other one.

"She is hungry," laughed Rhonda.

"Yes, she is." Aunt Joanne laughed too. "Here are two more for her."

"She is happy now," Rhonda said to Aunt Joanne as she took the crackers.

Aunt Joanne smiled at Rhonda. "You were a kind big sister, Rhonda," she said. "You helped Amy be happy, and that was a big help to me. Thank you."

"You are welcome," Rhonda said with a happy smile at Aunt Joanne. "I like to be a helper."

3.

Four Days With Aunt Joanne

Jesus Helps Valerie

Valerie stretched and opened her eyes. Sunlight was streaming in the window at the head of her bed. She looked around the little room. This was not her room! Where was she? Valerie buried her head in her pillow and began to sob. She did not like to be all alone in this strange room.

Aunt Joanne opened the bedroom door. "Oh, are you awake, Valerie?" she asked.

Valerie raised her head and looked at Aunt Joanne. Now she remembered. She was at Aunt Joanne's house.

"What's wrong, dear?" Aunt Joanne asked kindly, sitting down on the bed. She put her arm around Valerie. "Were you afraid?"

Valerie nodded. "Yes. I—I didn't know where I was."

"Now you know where you are, don't you," Aunt Joanne said kindly. "Rhonda got up about an hour ago. She is helping me make breakfast. Shall we dress you so you can eat with us too?"

"Yes," Valerie answered as she climbed out of bed. She was not afraid anymore. She let Aunt Joanne help her put on her dress and socks and shoes. Then they walked out to the kitchen.

Soon Aunt Joanne, Clarence, Rhonda, and Valerie were sitting at the table. They bowed their heads, and Aunt Joanne asked the blessing. "Bless Father and Mother while they are in Missouri," she prayed. "Be near to Glen's family and comfort them in their sorrow. Be with Clarence and Rhonda and Valerie and Amy. Help them to be happy and obedient today. In Jesus' Name. Amen."

"What are you going to do today, Aunt Joanne?" Rhonda asked as she helped herself to a piece of toast.

"This morning we will do the cleaning," Aunt Joanne answered. "I need some helpers. Rhonda, will you sweep the kitchen floor please? Clarence, you may gather all the wastebaskets and put the trash in the big bag in the laundry room. When you have all the trash in the bag, you may take it out to the garage."

"What may I do?" Valerie asked eagerly as soon as breakfast was over.

"Here is a dustcloth," Aunt Joanne said, handing it to her. "You may dust all the furniture in the living room. Be very careful that you don't knock things over."

"I will be careful," Valerie promised. She skipped to the living room with her dustcloth.

"'I'll do it all for Jesus; / I'll do it all for Jesus,'" she sang happily.

"Can someone please open the door for me?" Clarence called.

"I will!" Valerie ran to open the door.

"Thank you," Clarence said as he smiled at his little sister. "You are a good helper."

Just then a gust of wind blew in the open window. The door slammed shut with a *bang!*

"Ow-w-w!" Valerie screamed.

Aunt Joanne rushed over to help Valerie. Opening the door, she freed Valerie's finger that

had been pinched in the door. Blood dripped onto the floor.

Aunt Joanne carried Valerie to the bathroom. She washed the finger with a cold cloth, but it took a while before it stopped bleeding.

"Her fingernail is almost off," Aunt Joanne said, holding it out for Rhonda to see. "And she has a big cut right here."

Tears came to Rhonda's eyes. "Oh!" she exclaimed. "That must really hurt!"

"I think I should take her to the doctor," Aunt Joanne said. "This gash should probably have stitches. I'm going to call Grandma and see if she can come over to stay with the rest of you children while we go."

Aunt Joanne called Grandma. She came over right away. Soon Aunt Joanne and Valerie were on their way to the doctor.

"I don't want to go to the doctor!" Valerie cried as Aunt Joanne drove up to the big brick building. "Will he hurt me, Aunt Joanne?"

"Yes, it might hurt a little," Aunt Joanne said. "But remember that Jesus is with you, Valerie."

Valerie stopped crying and tried to smile. She still held tightly to Aunt Joanne's hand as they walked into the waiting room.

"You may come with me right away," the

nurse said when she saw them. She led them into a little room. She took Valerie's temperature and wrote some things down on a piece of paper. "The doctor will be in soon," she said.

Soon the doctor came in. "Hello, young lady," he said. "So you have a hurt finger?"

Valerie nodded.

The doctor looked at it. Then he walked over to his table and picked up several things.

Valerie's eyes got big as she looked at the needle the doctor held in his hand. "Is he going to give me a shot?" she asked Aunt Joanne fearfully.

"I will have to stick this needle in your arm," the doctor said kindly. "It will hurt a little, but it will soon be over. Then you will not be able to feel it when we sew up your finger."

Valerie held tightly to Aunt Joanne's hand as the doctor stuck the needle into her arm. Tears rolled down her face. The needle hurt. But it did not take long at all. Then the doctor sewed up her finger.

"It is not hurting," Valerie told Aunt Joanne with a little smile.

"Good," the doctor said. Then he told Aunt Joanne, "Her fingernail will probably come off, and a new one will grow.

"You were a brave girl," he said to Valerie. "You may choose two balloons from this box." He put a box in her lap. "What colors do you want?"

Valerie chose a blue balloon and a pink one. "Jesus helped me to be brave," she told the doctor.

"He certainly did," the doctor agreed.

Aunt Joanne paid the bill; then they walked to the car.

"I was afraid, Aunt Joanne," Valerie said as Aunt Joanne buckled her seat belt. "That needle hurt. But I asked God to help me to be brave, and He did!"

"I am glad you remembered to ask God to help you," Aunt Joanne said. "God always wants to help us, and He is pleased when we tell Him about our problems."

"When we get to your house, I'm going to tell Rhonda and Clarence how Jesus helped me," Valerie said.

"They will want to hear all about it," Aunt Joanne agreed as she turned the car toward home.

4.

Four Days With Aunt Joanne

A Friend for Valerie

Sunday morning arrived. Clarence stretched and yawned as he entered the kitchen. The sun was shining in the window at the sink, making the kitchen look bright and cheery.

"Good morning, Clarence," Aunt Joanne greeted him. She was standing at the kitchen sink, peeling potatoes.

"Good morning," Clarence returned as he sat down to tie his shoes.

"What do you usually have for breakfast on Sunday mornings?" Aunt Joanne asked as she sliced a potato into the casserole dish that was sitting on the counter.

"We usually have corn flakes, and toast with jam," Clarence told her. "Sometimes Mother makes sticky buns too."

"Well, I don't have any corn flakes, but I do have Cheerios," Aunt Joanne said. "And I think we'll have hot buttered rolls. Does that sound all right?"

"Oh, yes!" Clarence answered. "I like Cheerios even better than corn flakes."

"So do I," Rhonda added. She had just come out of her bedroom, and now she was sitting on the sofa tying her shoes.

Aunt Joanne was putting the rolls into the oven when Valerie came out of her bedroom too. She had tried to dress herself. Her stockings were on crooked, and her shoes were on the wrong feet.

"Oh, Valerie, you look funny!" Clarence exclaimed.

Valerie's mouth turned down, and she looked as though she were going to cry.

"Don't make fun of her, Clarence," Aunt Joanne said. "She did her very best. When you were her age, you made mistakes too when you tried to dress yourself. I remember one time when I was at your house and you came downstairs with your shirt buttoned crooked and your pants on backwards."

Clarence smiled sheepishly. That had been so long ago that he did not remember it at all. "I'm sorry, Valerie," he said. "I know you did your best."

Valerie's face became sunny again. She let Aunt Joanne zip up her dress. Then Aunt Joanne straightened her socks and put her shoes on the right feet.

"Now you're all fixed up," Aunt Joanne said cheerily. "And it's time to set the table."

Aunt Joanne got the plates and glasses down for Rhonda. Clarence went to the silverware drawer and began to count out four knives, four forks, and four spoons. Aunt Joanne got Cheerios out of the cupboard and milk from the refrigerator. Soon they were ready to eat.

"We are going to have visitors for dinner," Aunt Joanne told the children while they were eating. "They are from Illinois, and their mother was in my grade at school when we were little girls. They will go to another church this morning, but then they will come to our house for dinner. They have five children. There are twin boys about Clarence's age and a girl a little older

34

than Valerie. Then there are two younger boys."

"Oh, Valerie will like to play with the little girl," Rhonda said, smiling at her little sister.

Valerie nodded her head vigorously.

"I want to tell you something, children," Aunt Joanne said. "The little girl's name is Sara Ann, and she is one of God's special children. She can't walk, and her hands are crippled. But inside her crippled body is a dear little girl just like you."

Rhonda's brow creased in a puzzled frown. "But how can we play with her if she can't walk?"

"You can give her a doll to hold," Aunt Joanne suggested. "And if you want to play church, we could line up chairs in my bedroom. Then Sara Ann can sit with you in her wheelchair."

"Okay," Rhonda said.

"Okay," Valerie agreed. "I like to play church!"

When breakfast was over, Aunt Joanne quickly washed the dishes, and Clarence dried them. Then Aunt Joanne helped the children finish getting ready for church.

"I'm not used to getting five people ready for church." Aunt Joanne laughed as she ran the comb through Clarence's hair. "Do you think I know how to do it right?"

"Oh, I think so," Rhonda answered. "You just have to comb my hair yet, and then we'll all be ready, won't we?"

"I think so," Aunt Joanne answered. Before long everyone was ready, and Aunt Joanne hustled them out the door.

When church was over that morning, Aunt Joanne and the children were soon on their way home. When they arrived, Clarence and Rhonda helped Aunt Joanne set the table for company.

"They're here!" Valerie called from the window where she had been watching. "And there is Sara Ann. Her father is putting her in her wheelchair."

Aunt Joanne wiped her hands on the kitchen towel and walked to the door to welcome the guests. She greeted the mother with a holy kiss and shook hands with the father and the children.

"Hello, what's your name?" Sara Ann's mother asked, shaking hands with Valerie.

"Valerie," Valerie answered shyly.

"And are you about four years old?" Sara Ann's mother asked.

Valerie shook her head.

"She will have a birthday soon," Rhonda said. "Then she will be four."

"Sara Ann is four already," her mother said. "Sara Ann, can you shake hands with Valerie?"

Sara Ann reached out her hand, but Valerie drew back behind Aunt Joanne's skirt. She had never seen such a crippled hand before.

"Shake hands with Sara Ann," Aunt Joanne encouraged her.

Slowly Valerie reached out and shook Sara Ann's hand. Sara Ann smiled at Valerie, but Valerie was too frightened to smile back.

When dinner was over, Aunt Joanne set up chairs in the bedroom for the girls to play church. Rhonda carefully pushed Sara Ann's wheelchair over to the chairs.

While the others were getting the "church" ready, Valerie quietly slipped away. She ran to the bedroom where she and Rhonda slept and crawled under the bed.

"Aunt Joanne, where is Valerie?" Rhonda asked. "We are ready to have church, but I can't find Valerie."

"I don't know," Aunt Joanne answered. She looked around, but she could not see Valerie either. Then she went into the other rooms to

look. Finally she came to the girls' bedroom. There she heard a sniffle. It sounded as though it was coming from under the bed. Aunt Joanne bent down and looked.

"Why, Valerie!" she exclaimed. "Come here and tell Aunt Joanne what is wrong."

Slowly Valerie crawled out from under the bed. Aunt Joanne sat down on the bed and pulled Valerie onto her lap.

Valerie laid her head on Aunt Joanne's shoulder. "I—I'm s-scared of that little girl," she sobbed. "She looks so—so funny."

"I know she looks different than the other children you are used to," Aunt Joanne said. "But tell me, Valerie, who made you?"

"God did," Valerie said with a sniffle.

"Who made Sara Ann?"

"God," Valerie answered again.

"Do you look just the same as your friends Donna and Carol?" Aunt Joanne asked next.

Slowly Valerie shook her head.

"No, you don't," Aunt Joanne said. "None of us look exactly the same. God has a plan for each of us, and He made us in the special way that He wants us to be. God made Sara Ann special too. She is a very sweet little girl, and you do not need to be afraid of her. Will you go now and play nicely with her?" Aunt Joanne wiped the tears from Valerie's cheeks with a hanky.

"Yes, I will," Valerie said. She slid off Aunt Joanne's lap and ran to play with the other girls.

Valerie sat down beside Sara Ann's wheelchair. "I like you," she whispered, touching Sara Ann's hand. She smiled at Sara Ann, and Sara Ann smiled back. Valerie was not afraid anymore. She wanted to be Sara Ann's friend.

5.

Four Days With Aunt Joanne

Father and Mother Come Home

"Is today the day that Father and Mother come home?" Rhonda asked as she entered the kitchen on Monday morning.

"Yes, it is," Aunt Joanne replied. She was standing at the stove, frying pancakes for breakfast. "You will be glad to see Father and Mother again, won't you?"

"Yes!" Rhonda answered. "I like it at your house, but I can hardly wait for Father and Mother to come home."

"I understand," Aunt Joanne said kindly.

"That is the way God meant it to be. He meant for fathers and mothers and children to enjoy being at home together. Because you love your father and mother, you miss them when they are gone. That is the way it should be.

"I remember one time when I was just a little older than Clarence," Aunt Joanne continued. "Mother let me go to my grandma's house for three days. I always liked to visit my grandma, and I was sure I would have lots of fun there for three whole days. Grandma made sure that I had a good time, but when Father came for me, I was so happy to see him. I decided that I never, never wanted to go away again for such a long time!"

Rhonda laughed. "But now you don't live with your father and mother anymore."

"No," Aunt Joanne answered. "It is God's will for most boys and girls to grow up and to have their own homes. God did not give me a husband and children to share my home with. But He has given me a nice home here close to Grandpa's. And sometimes I can share my home with my nieces and nephews."

Clarence came into the kitchen holding up a button. "Aunt Joanne, a button came off my shirt," he said. "See?"

"Yes, I see," Aunt Joanne said. "Well, breakfast is almost ready. Let's eat, and then I'll sew that button on for you."

When breakfast was over and the dishes had been washed, Aunt Joanne sewed the button on Clarence's shirt. Then she sat down at the sewing machine.

"What are you sewing, Aunt Joanne?" Rhonda asked.

"I am sewing a dress for your friend Katrina," Aunt Joanne answered. "Katrina's mother is very busy, and she asked me if I would sew some dresses for the girls."

Rhonda fingered the piece of material that Aunt Joanne was holding. "This is just like the dress that Mother is making for me!" Rhonda's eyes shone. "Katrina and I will have dresses alike!"

"Won't that be nice!" Aunt Joanne smiled at Rhonda.

The day passed as the children played and helped Aunt Joanne. Finally suppertime came. The children enjoyed Aunt Joanne's chicken noodle soup and grilled cheese sandwiches.

"Are Father and Mother coming soon?" Clarence asked as he began drying the dishes after supper.

"They said they should be here around six-thirty," Aunt Joanne answered. "That will be about another hour. Would you like to play a game of Candy Land when the dishes are done?"

"Yes, let's!" Clarence replied.

"Rhonda, you may get out the Candy Land game," Aunt Joanne said. "Clarence and I are almost done with the dishes."

Rhonda hurried to get the game. Placing it on the table, she opened the box and took out the board. "Which of the gingerbread men do you want, Clarence?" she asked.

"Give me the blue one," Clarence said. "I like him best."

"Which one do you want, Aunt Joanne?"

"Either one is fine," she said.

"Okay, and I'll take the red one," Rhonda said. "Aunt Joanne may have the green one or the yellow one."

"I'll take the green one," Aunt Joanne said with a smile.

Clarence wiped the last plate and set it carefully on the counter. He hopped off his stool and carried it to the corner of the kitchen, where it belonged. Then he hurried over to the table and sat down. Aunt Joanne soon came and joined them.

"May I help too?" Valerie asked, coming into the kitchen.

"Me too," Amy added, toddling over to Aunt Joanne.

"Yes, Valerie, you may help. Rhonda, why don't you help Valerie with her turns. Amy may help me," Aunt Joanne said. She swung Amy up onto her lap.

"Who's going to go first?" Clarence asked.

"Let's let Valerie go first this time," Aunt Joanne suggested.

They had all taken their first turns when there was a *cru-unch* on the gravel outside.

"I think I hear a car," Aunt Joanne said. "Do you think that's Father and Mother already?"

"I hope not," Clarence said. "I want to finish this game first."

Rhonda jumped up to look out the window. "It *is* them!" she squealed. She flung the door open and ran outside to meet Mother and Father. Valerie followed her.

Amy slid down from Aunt Joanne's lap and toddled toward the door. "Mama! Mama!" she cried. Aunt Joanne got up and walked to the door to meet Father and Mother too.

Only Clarence stayed at the table. His mouth turned into a pout. "Can't we finish this

game, Aunt Joanne?" he pleaded.

"I don't think so, Clarence," Aunt Joanne answered. "Father and Mother will probably want to go soon."

Mother came in the door with Rhonda holding tightly to one hand and Valerie to her other one. Father followed, and he scooped up Amy, who was reaching up her chubby arms, to be held.

"Hello, Clarence. Is there something wrong? You don't look very happy," Father said, looking at Clarence's sad face.

"I wanted to finish this game before you came," Clarence said, his face still looking like a storm cloud. "But Aunt Joanne said we can't finish it now."

"That's right," Father said. "It's time to go home. Put the game away now."

Unhappily, Clarence dumped the gingerbread men off the board and slammed the board together.

"Clarence, come with me," Father said, taking his son's arm and leading him to the laundry room.

Closing the door, Father said, "We cannot let you act like this when you are disappointed, Clarence. I know you were hoping to finish the game, but now your plans have changed, yet you must be cheerful. All of us are disappointed sometimes, even grownups. God wants us to learn to accept disappointments cheerfully. I will have to punish you for pouting and for getting so upset."

Father spanked Clarence. When Clarence stopped crying, Father said, "Now let's go back to the kitchen. I want you to put the game away. And I think you should tell Aunt Joanne you are sorry for pouting."

Father and Clarence went back to the kitchen. Clarence put the gingerbread men and the cards and the board neatly into the box and closed it.

Aunt Joanne came out of the spare bedroom, carrying the girls' suitcase.

"I'm sorry I pouted, Aunt Joanne," Clarence said. He looked up at Aunt Joanne's kind face and then down at his shoes.

"I forgive you," Aunt Joanne said kindly.

Father picked up two suitcases and headed toward the door. Clarence walked beside him out to the car.

That night when Father tucked Clarence into bed, Clarence said, "I'm glad you came home, Father. I like it at Aunt Joanne's house, but home is best of all!"

"Mother and I are glad to be home too," Father said, giving Clarence a good-night kiss. "God planned for families, and He planned that home should be a happy place where we like to be. We are glad for God's special plan, aren't we?"

"Yes," Clarence mumbled sleepily. He rolled over and was soon fast asleep.

6.

Troubles in the Workshop

"Good-bye, Father!" six-year-old David called as Father got into his pickup to leave for work.

"Good-bye, David," Father replied. "Be good for Mother today."

"I will," David promised. Then he turned and raced back to the house.

"Mother, what are you going to do today?" David asked.

"First of all the dishes need to be washed, and I need a helper," Mother replied with a smile. "Then I need to bake bread and work on the mending pile. We should pull weeds some-time today too. Maybe we can do that this after-noon."

David got his little stool and placed it at the sink. Washing the breakfast dishes was usually his job. There were not very many dishes, and soon he was done.

"Mother, may I go out to the shop?" he asked when his job was finished.

"Yes, you may," Mother replied, "but remem-ber not to play with Father's tools."

"I'll remember," David promised. He ran out-side.

"I like the little corner that Father fixed for me," David thought as he opened the shop door. Right by the door Father had set up a little place for David to have his shop. He had a little table for a workbench. A little tool set that Grandpa and Grandma had given him for his birthday sat on the table. Father often gave him wood scraps to make things with. David loved to spend time in his shop.

But he remembered what Father had said. "You must never, never use my big tools when I'm not in the shop," Father had warned. "They are too dangerous for little boys. If I ever find that you played anywhere besides in your corner, you won't be allowed to be in the shop at all while I am away."

David did not want that to happen. He wanted to obey Father. He liked to play in his little shop while Father was at work.

"I'm going to make a little box to put my smallest scraps of wood in," David decided. He picked out some of the biggest scrap pieces and began to nail them together.

David spent the whole morning in his shop. First he made his box. Then he took a chunk of wood and pounded four nails into it. He was busy with that job when Mother stuck her head in the door. "May I come in?" she asked.

"Sure." David grinned. "I always like company."

"What are you making?" Mother asked, looking at his piece of wood.

"These nails are going to be hooks to hang things on," David explained. "I'm going to ask Father to help me put it here on the wall."

"That sounds like a good idea," Mother approved. She looked around a bit more in his shop. Then she went back to the house.

The morning went fast, and before David knew it, Mother was calling, "David! Come in. It is lunchtime!"

David put his tools neatly back into his tool chest. Then he ran to the house.

After dinner it was nap time. Mother read a story, and then David lay down on the couch. Mother took baby Sara and went to the bedroom.

When David's nap time was over, he announced, "I'm going outside to the sandbox."

"All right," Mother answered.

After a while David heard Mother calling, "David!"

David got up and brushed the sand from his pants. "What, Mother?"

"I want you to come and help me pull weeds in the garden," Mother said.

David ran to Mother. Soon he was busy pulling weeds in the onion row. Mother worked nearby hoeing corn. They were still working in the garden when Father came home from work.

"Well, it looks like we have some busy people out here," Father said as he walked over to the garden. "David, I'm glad to see you being Mother's cheerful helper."

David beamed. Father's praise made him happy inside.

Father took his lunch box to the house. Then

David saw him heading toward the shop. Father usually worked in his shop for a while in the afternoons.

Before long, Father came out of the shop again. He walked toward the garden.

"David," Father called, "were you in my part of the shop today?"

"Why, no, Father. I just stayed in my own little part the way you told me to," David answered. "Why?"

"Come with me," Father instructed.

David followed Father to the shop. He knew that he had obeyed. He wondered what Father wanted to show him.

"Look," Father said when they were inside the shop. "My hammer is lying on the floor, and this box of nails is spilled. What happened?"

"I—I don't know," David answered. "I didn't see that before."

Father put his hand under David's chin and made David look up at him. "Are you sure you don't know anything about it, son?"

"I'm sure," David answered.

"Let's go and ask Mother about it," Father decided. "Maybe she knows something."

But Mother did not know anything about it either. "As far as I know, only David was in the

56

shop today," she said. "I went to check on him this morning. He was busy in his little corner then. I didn't see anything out of order. But maybe something happened since then."

"I want to believe you, David," Father said kindly. "But something happened in the shop. Maybe we should decide that tomorrow you will stay out of the shop. That will give us a little time to find out what happened out there today.

"Of course, you know, David, that it is wrong to disobey. If you tell a lie about it, that makes it much worse."

David's eyes filled with tears. He did not know what had happened in Father's shop. He felt very sad that Father thought that maybe he had disobeyed. How could he make Father believe that he had not done it?

That night at bedtime Father and David prayed together beside David's bed as they usually did. Then Father tucked David into his bed. When Father had turned out the light, David buried his face in his pillow. "Dear God," he prayed, "please help Father to know what happened in his shop. I didn't do it, and I don't know who did. In Jesus' Name. Amen." David felt much better, and soon he fell asleep.

The next morning David was awake early. "Today I can't play in the shop at all," he thought sadly as he sat up in his bed. The shop was one of his favorite places to play.

Just then Father opened the door a crack. "David, are you awake?" he asked. He stepped into the room.

"Uncle Jonathan called last night after you were asleep," Father told David.

David nodded and waited for Father to go on. What was Father going to say?

"He said that he stopped in yesterday afternoon," Father continued. "He had broken one of his drill bits, and he needed it to finish a job he was doing for a customer. He decided to borrow one I have that is just like it. The house seemed very quiet, so he thought maybe you and Mother were napping. So he just went into the shop and found the drill bit. He was in a big hurry, and he happened to dump the box of nails. The hammer fell down too. He said he should have picked them up, but his customer was in a big hurry to have the job finished."

David's face lighted up. "Oh, I'm so glad!" he exclaimed. "I mean, I'm glad that we found out who it was."

"Yes," Father said, laying his hand on David's shoulder. "I'm glad too. The Lord knew what happened in the shop and helped us to find out."

David threw his arms around Father's neck. "I'm so glad God helped us, Father."

"Yes," Father said. "So am I. I'm glad that

our David is a truthful little boy." Father gave him a special smile.

David smiled too. He was not sad anymore. "May I play in my shop today, Father?" he asked.

"Yes, you may," Father answered with a smile. "And now it's time to get up and get dressed. Mother has breakfast almost ready."

"Do we have time to pray and thank God for helping you to find out who was in your shop?" David asked. "I prayed last night when I was in bed that God would help you know who did it."

"Yes, we can do that," Father agreed. "I am glad you want to thank God for answering your prayer. God is pleased when we remember to thank Him when He helps us."

David jumped out of bed and knelt beside Father. "Dear God," he prayed, "thank You for helping Father to know who was in his shop. Thank You for a happy day, and help us to trust You all the time. In Jesus' Name. Amen."

Then Father prayed too. "Dear Father in heaven," he prayed, "thank You for letting me know what happened in the shop. Thank You that our little boy was obedient. Help us always to do what is right. In Jesus' Name. Amen."

David hurried to get dressed. "'I'm H-A-P-P-Y, I'm H-A-P-P-Y, / I know I am, I'm sure I am, / I'm H-A-P-P-Y,'" he sang as he hopped down the stairs. He knew that this was going to be a happy day because the problem had been solved and everything was right again.

7.

The Spill in the Shop

"Father, may I make a little boat for Brother Jonathan's birthday?" David asked one Saturday morning. Brother Jonathan lived by himself in a trailer close to David's family. David and his parents often went to visit him. Brother Jonathan had told David that he was going to be eighty-nine years old on Monday.

"Why, yes, I think that would be a nice idea," Father answered. "Would you like for me to cut out the pieces for you?"

"Oh, yes!" David's eyes shone.

Father took several pieces of scraps from David's box. David watched as Father drew lines and then sawed off the pieces to make the right shapes.

"Someday I'll be able to do that all by myself," David said. "I wish I was big enough to do it now."

Father smiled. "That time will come in just a few years, the Lord willing. I'm happy that our little boy is growing up. But don't be in too big of a hurry. We would like to have a little boy for a while yet! God wants us to be content and happy right now too."

David smiled and nodded as Father handed him the pieces of wood.

"Now," Father said, "I need to go to the house to study for my sermon tomorrow. Do you think you can nail those pieces together?"

"I think so," David answered.

"Just do the best you can," Father encouraged. "I am sure Brother Jonathan will be happy to have a gift that you made yourself. Maybe I can help you paint it this afternoon."

Father left the shop, and David was all by himself. He held two of the pieces together carefully and looked at them.

"I think I'll need those smaller nails," David

decided. He laid down his hammer and walked over to the shelf in the corner, where he had a box of tiny nails that Father had given him. He sang lustily, "When my cup runneth over with J-O-Y, / When my cup runneth over with J-O-Y, / I find it easy to pray / And to sing all the day . . ."

As David reached up to get the box of nails, his foot accidentally kicked against something. As he turned to look, he gasped in dismay.

A can of oil that had been sitting nearby had tipped over. The lid had come off, and a pool of oil was spreading over the floor.

"Oh, what shall I do?" David asked aloud. Quickly David set the can upright. "Father won't like it that his oil is spilled." There was still a little bit of oil in the bottom, but most of it was on the floor.

"I should clean it up," David thought. "But what shall I clean it up with?"

He looked around a little and soon found two old rags under his worktable. He took them over to the corner and began wiping the spill. But it was a hard job. The oil was mixed with dust from the floor, and it was a sticky mess. Besides, David was not feeling at all happy. He was in trouble and needed help.

Suddenly David decided, "I must tell Father what happened. I am sure that is what he would want me to do."

David laid down his rag and headed toward the house.

Mother was folding wash at the kitchen table. "Why, David, what happened to you?" she exclaimed when she saw his greasy hands and pants.

"I—I—" David began. He looked down at the floor. "I spilled some oil in the shop," he said quietly. "It was an accident, but it made a mess."

"You'd better put different pants on right away," Mother said. "I'll need to scrub these, and we don't want oil on other things here in the house."

Mother helped David scrub his hands and change his pants.

"Mother, do you think Father is very busy studying?" David asked when he was clean again. "I should tell him about the spill, shouldn't I?"

"Yes, you should, David," Mother answered. "Just a minute. I will tell him you want to talk to him and see if it suits him."

Mother knocked on Father's study door. "May David come in? He has something he wants to tell you."

"Sure," Father answered. He smiled as David slowly entered the study. "Are you having a problem, son?"

"I—I spilled a can of oil in the shop," David answered. "I'm sorry, Father. I didn't mean to. I just happened to kick it over when I was getting my nails."

Father laid down his pen. "We'd better go and clean it up," he said.

David followed Father out to the shop. Father noticed the oily rags that David had been using.

"Did you try to clean it up?" Father asked.

David nodded. "I thought maybe I wouldn't have to tell you about it," he confessed. "I thought maybe I could just wipe it up. But I couldn't get the floor clean. And—and I knew I really should tell you anyway."

"You did the right thing by coming and telling me about it, David," Father said kindly. "When you make a mistake, never try to cover it up. Instead, tell Father or Mother about it so that we can help you fix it.

"What you did was not bad. It was just an accident. But if you had cleaned it up so that I wouldn't know what happened, that would have been wrong. Sometimes children even tell lies because they don't want their parents to find out what happened. They might not tell their parents about it for many years. Then they have much unhappiness because they do not talk to their parents. Always remember that the right way is to tell Father or Mother right away."

"I will try," David said soberly. He knew that he had done what was right. He knew that he should never try to hide his mistakes from his parents.

"Now let's clean up this mess," Father said.

It did not take Father long to clean up the mess with a bucket of soapy water, a scrub brush, and a rag.

"Thank you, Father," David said when Father stood up.

"You're welcome," Father said with a smile. "Now I'd better get back to the house to finish studying for my sermon."

8.

God Planned Our Family

Rachel picked up another dish from the drainer and began drying it. "Mother, is Rosetta really all ours now?" she asked. She looked at her baby sister, who was lying on her stomach on the floor.

Rosetta heard her name. She looked up at Rachel and gurgled happily. Rachel smiled back. She loved her little sister.

"Yes, she is all ours now." Mother's voice was happy. She and Father had been to many adoption meetings. There had been papers to sign and telephone calls to make. But finally little Rosetta, who had come to live with their family three months before, was "all theirs."

"I'm glad." Rachel's eyes sparkled. "Now we have seven children in our family. I like seven."

"Seven children is a nice number, isn't it." Mother smiled at Rachel. "We are happy to have seven children. And if the Lord ever blesses us with more, we will thank Him for each of them too."

"I remember when we adopted Wendy," Rachel said. "I was five years old then. I was the youngest in our family, and I was so happy to have a little sister. Wendy was three years old when we adopted her, wasn't she, Mother?"

"Yes, that's right," Mother answered. "That was two years ago. Now Wendy is five years old, and you are seven."

The next morning, Mother shook her sleepy daughter. "Rachel, it's time to get up," she said. "Remember, we want to go to Mountain View Church this morning. It will take us an hour to get there."

After breakfast, Father and Mother helped the children finish getting ready to go to church.

"Here, Wendy, let me tie your shoes," Father

said. Wendy sat on a chair and held up first one foot and then the other.

"Rachel, will you please get Rosetta's cap and sweater?" Mother requested. Rachel hurried to obey.

"Everyone out to the van," Father called. When they were outside, Father locked the door and followed the others to the van.

An hour later they arrived at the Mountain View Church. "Thank God for a safe trip," Father announced as he turned the van in the driveway.

Rachel and Wendy followed Mother as she walked into the church house carrying baby Rosetta. The four boys went with Father. Soon they were all seated in the auditorium, waiting for the service to begin.

When the service was over, Rachel pulled on Mother's sleeve. "Mother, may I hold Rosetta?" she asked.

"Sure," Mother answered. She handed Rosetta to Rachel. Rachel sat down on the bench with Rosetta.

A girl named Sandra left her mother's side and walked over to Rachel. Rachel knew Sandra because she had visited their church one time. Sandra was nine years old.

"I'm glad you came to our church today," Sandra said.

Rachel smiled. "I'm glad too," she said. "I have never been here before."

Sandra patted Rosetta's hand. "Is this your baby sister?" she asked.

Rachel nodded. "Her name is Rosetta."

A puzzled look came over Sandra's face. "But she doesn't look like you," she said. "She doesn't look like your mother and father either. Her skin is dark and her hair is curly. White mothers and fathers always have white babies."

"She is adopted," Rachel explained.

"Oh," Sandra said. "So she isn't really your sister?"

"Yes, she is my sister," Rachel said. "She is my sister because we adopted her."

"But she's not really your sister if she wasn't born in your family," Sandra said.

"But Mother said she is our own baby now," Rachel said. "All the papers are finished and everything, so she belongs in our family now."

"Anyway, she is a sweet baby," Sandra said. "May I hold her?"

Rachel looked up at Mother. "May Sandra hold Rosetta?" she asked.

Mother smiled at the girls. "Yes, she may hold Rosetta if she sits down beside you."

Sandra sat down beside Rachel and held out her hands toward Rosetta. Rosetta smiled and reached out her chubby arms.

"She likes me," Sandra said. She touched Rosetta on her nose, and Rosetta giggled.

When they were on the way home, Rachel burst out, "Mother, do you know what?"

"No, what, dear?" Mother asked, looking at Rachel.

"Sandra asked me if Rosetta is my baby sister, and I said she is." Rachel paused. "But then she noticed that Rosetta doesn't look like us, and so I told her she is adopted. Then Sandra said that Rosetta isn't really my sister if she wasn't born in our family. That's not true, is it, Mother?"

Mother smiled kindly at Rachel. "Rosetta is all ours now because we adopted her. You and the boys are special in our family because you were born in our family. Wendy and Rosetta are special because they were adopted. Some people may tell you that Rosetta isn't really your sister. But usually they do not mean to be unkind. We must forgive them and be kind to them. And we will still have a happy family, won't we, Rachel?"

"Yes." Rachel nodded.

"God had a plan for Rosetta when she was born," Father said. "He had a plan for our family too. He knew that our family wanted another baby, and I believe He brought Rosetta to us. When Rosetta was born, God knew that she would become part of our family."

Rachel nodded. "I'm glad God planned for Rosetta to be part of our family," she said. "She is a dear baby sister. And Sandra said she is sweet too."

Rosetta was sitting in her car seat beside Rachel. She turned her head and smiled at Rachel. Rachel smiled back. "I think Rosetta knows that we are talking about her." She leaned over and kissed Rosetta's cheek. "I love you, and I'm glad God planned for you to be a part of our family," she whispered.

"Da-da," Rosetta said, clapping her hands.

"I think she's saying 'I'm glad too,'" Rachel giggled.

"We're all glad that God planned our happy family," Mother said as Father drove the van in the lane.

9.

Brave Like Daniel

"There's Galen waiting for you," Father said to Harold as they turned in the driveway at the Weber home. Galen was sitting on the swing, slowly swinging back and forth. As soon as Father stopped the car, Harold jumped out and ran over to Galen.

"I'm so glad you could come," Galen said happily. "Eugene's family is coming too. Father said that we may play in my tree house after dinner."

"Good!" Harold exclaimed. "I like your tree

house. That will be fun!"

Soon Eugene's family arrived, and Eugene joined the two boys.

"Let's play on the swings until Mother calls for dinner," Galen suggested. "You boys can swing, and I'll push you."

"Okay," Harold and Eugene agreed. Soon they were both whizzing through the air. Galen pushed Harold first, then Eugene, and then Harold again.

"Boys! Dinner!" Galen's mother called a few minutes later. The three boys hurried to the house. They washed their hands and then sat down at the table. Harold enjoyed the delicious turkey, noodles, and corn. But he was glad when dinner was over and Galen's father said they were excused.

"Are we going to play in the tree house now?" Harold asked when they were outside.

"Yes, let's," Galen answered. "Come along."

The three boys ran to the big maple tree. Soon they were sitting on the floor of the tree house.

"What can we do up here?" Eugene wondered.

"The last time I was here, Galen brought his farm set up here to the tree house," Harold said.

"It was crowded, but we had fun. But it might not work so well with three boys."

Eugene stood up and looked out the tree house window. "Oh, look, someone is coming! He's walking on the road, and I think he has a cane. Who is it, Galen?"

Galen looked out the window too. "That's

our neighbor man, Mr. Smith," he answered. "He walks past here almost every day. I think he goes to the little store up the road to buy his groceries."

"On Sundays too?" Eugene wondered.

"Yes," Galen answered. "Mr. Smith isn't a Christian. Father talks to him sometimes about the Bible. Sometimes Father also invites him to church, but he always says, 'Maybe sometime.'"

Eugene watched the old man hobble closer. "I know what!" he suggested. "Let's go over to that bush by the road. When he comes past, let's jump up and make faces at him."

Harold did not think that sounded like a very nice idea, but he did not want to say no. He looked at Galen. Galen was slowly following Eugene, who had started down the ladder. So Harold climbed down too.

The three boys hurried over to the bush and crouched down. Harold saw that Galen did not look very happy. Harold did not feel happy either.

"I don't think we should do this," Galen said. "Father teaches me to be kind to old people. One time I made fun of Mr. Smith's big ears, and Father punished me. I'm not going to help."

He jumped up and started back toward the tree house.

"I'm not going to help either," Harold said. He got up and followed Galen.

"Come on, boys," Eugene whispered. "We aren't going to hurt him."

Galen shook his head. "No," he said firmly.

"Okay then," Eugene said. He got up slowly.

"I know what," Galen suggested. "Let's sing for Mr. Smith as he walks by."

By now, Mr. Smith was very close.

"Let's sing 'I Have a Wonderful Treasure,'" Harold suggested.

Together the boys began to sing, "'I have a wonderful treasure, / The gift of God without measure, / And so we travel together, / My Bible and I.'"

Mr. Smith stopped to listen. When that song was finished, the boys sang "The Wise Man and the Foolish Man" and then "Jesus Loves Me."

Soon Mr. Smith continued slowly on his way. The boys went back to the tree house.

It did not seem long to Harold until his father came and said, "Come. It's time to go home, Harold."

On the way home, Father asked, "And what did you boys do this afternoon?"

"We played in Galen's tree house," Harold said. "And do you know what, Father? Mr. Smith, their old neighbor man, walked by. Eugene wanted to hide behind the bushes and then jump up and make faces at him."

Father turned his head and looked at Harold. "And did you do that?"

"We went out to the bushes, but Galen and I weren't happy. Then Galen said he didn't want to help. He said his father punished him one time for making fun of Mr. Smith's ears."

"Then what did you do?" Father questioned.

"I said I didn't want to help either," Harold answered. "Eugene didn't like it at first, but then he decided not to do it either. Galen said we could sing for Mr. Smith, so we did."

Father looked pleased. "Galen was a good friend," he said. "When our friends do wrong, it is not easy to say no. In the Bible, I am sure it was not easy for Daniel to say no when most of his friends ate the king's meat. But he did what God wanted him to, and God blessed him. Galen was brave like Daniel, and he helped you and Eugene to do right too. The next time one of your friends wants to do something wrong, I want you to be brave like Galen was. Will you do that, Harold?"

"I will try," Harold said. "I want to be a good friend like Galen was."

"God is pleased when we help each other do right," Father said. "I am glad you sang for Mr. Smith. Maybe that will help him to think about God."

"I hope so," Harold said. "I want Mr. Smith to become a Christian."

"We must pray for him," Father said as he gave Harold a warm smile.

10.

Why Am I So Small?

"'Jesus loves me! This I know, / For the Bible tells me so . . .'" Elsie sang softly to Beth, her doll. She was giving Beth a bottle and rocking her to sleep.

Soon Beth was asleep. Elsie got up and softly walked to the doll's crib. She laid Beth in the crib and tucked the covers carefully around her. "Sleep tight, baby," she said.

"Beth is sleeping," she thought. "Now what can I do?"

Elsie wandered into the sewing room, where

big sister Susan sat at the sewing machine.

"What are you making?" Elsie asked, standing beside Susan.

"A dress for Ruthie," Susan answered, smiling at Elsie. Ruthie was Elsie's little niece.

"That is a pretty dress," Elsie said, fingering the light blue material. "May I help you?"

"I'm afraid you can't," Susan answered. "It would be too hard for you. When you are bigger, then you can sew dresses."

Sadly Elsie left the sewing room and walked out to the kitchen. Fifteen-year-old Ruby sat at the table with her typewriter.

"What are you typing, Ruby?" Elsie asked, sitting on a chair beside her big sister.

"I'm typing a report for school," Ruby answered.

"May I type?" Elsie asked.

"No, I have to get this assignment finished for school. When you are bigger, then you can learn to type too," Ruby answered. She smiled at Elsie and then began typing again.

Tears filled Elsie's eyes as she walked back to the living room. Mother came out of her bedroom. "Why, Elsie, what's wrong?" she asked kindly, seeing Elsie's sad face.

"Mother, why is everyone else big and I'm

so small?" Elsie cried.

"Why do you ask that, Elsie?" Mother asked in surprise.

"Well, Susan is making a dress for Ruthie, and I asked if I could help her. She said I have to wait till I'm bigger. And Ruby is typing a paper for school. She said I have to wait till I'm bigger to learn to type. Why am I so much littler than everybody, Mother?"

Mother took Elsie's hand and led her to the sofa. "Did you know that there is a verse in the Bible that talks about that?" she asked, taking Elsie onto her lap. "Matthew 6:27 says, 'Which of you by taking thought can add one cubit unto his stature?' That means, Which of you by thinking about it can make yourself taller? Of course, none of us can. God made us the way He wants us to be.

"God gave Father and me three little girls," Mother continued. "Those three little girls were Linda, Susan, and Ruby. We loved our three little girls and tried to teach them about God and the Bible. But our three little girls were getting bigger, and we wanted another little baby. Linda and Susan and Ruby often prayed that God would give them a little brother or sister if it was His will.

"When Ruby was six years old, God answered our prayers. A little baby came to live with us."

"Was it me?" Elsie asked eagerly.

"No, it wasn't you," Mother answered. "This baby was a boy, and his name was Edwin. But when Edwin was only four months old—about as old as Ruthie is now—he became very sick. Soon God took our dear little Edwin to heaven."

"Were you sad, Mother?" Elsie asked.

"Yes, we were very sad," Mother answered. "We missed little Edwin very much. But we knew that he was happy with God in heaven.

"Four more years went by, and then a baby girl came to live with us. Can you guess who that baby was?"

Elsie giggled. "Me!"

"That's right," Mother answered. "So you were a *very* special answer to our prayers. We all thanked God many times for sending you to us, and we still do." Mother hugged Elsie. "We are glad for our little girl that's so much younger."

Elsie smiled as she laid her head on Mother's shoulder. "I'm glad God answered your prayer," she said.

"So am I," Mother said. "And now I'll tell you something else. You can't make a dress for Ruthie, but would you like to do another job for me?"

Elsie nodded eagerly.

"When Sister Ann and little Carlos were here on Friday, Carlos was playing with the blue beads, and the string broke. Someone needs to put the beads on a new string," Mother said. "I think we should also put the red beads on a new string. That string is old too, and it might break soon. I will get the things for you, and you can do that for me. That's a job a little girl can do."

Mother got the beads and two new strings. "See, you put one dark blue bead on, then two light blue ones and then a dark one again." Mother put several beads on the string to show Elsie how to do it. "Do you understand?"

"I think so," Elsie answered, reaching for the beads. She put several more beads on the string while Mother stood and watched.

"Very good," Mother approved. "I believe you can do it yourself now. I need to go and start dinner. When you are finished with the blue one, call me, and I will help you start with the red one." Mother walked to the kitchen.

Elsie sat happily at the table, stringing the beads. She was glad that there were jobs for little people to do. She was glad that Mother had told her about God's answer to their prayers. "I won't mind being so much younger anymore," she thought.

11.

Edward Prays for Roger

"Edward, I want to go to Brother Virgil's this morning," Mother said. "Sister Rhoda wants to help me sew a covering."

"Oh, good!" Edward's eyes shone. "I like to go to Brother Virgil's. Their big boy, Roger, is nice. The last time we were there, he helped me build a tunnel in the hay."

"Roger might need to work today," Mother replied. "You must not keep him from his work. But if he wants to do things with you, that is all right."

Soon Mother and Edward were on their way to Brother Virgil's house. When they arrived, Sister Rhoda met them at the door and welcomed them in.

"Where is Roger?" Edward asked.

"He's out in the barn," Sister Rhoda replied. "I think he's cleaning out the sheep pen. Do you know where that is?"

"Yes, I know!" Edward answered. "Roger showed me the lambs when we were here the last time. May I go and find him?"

"Yes, you may," Sister Rhoda answered.

Edward hurried out to the barn. It did not take him long to find Roger in the sheep pen.

"Why, who comes here?" Roger teased as he threw a forkful of manure onto the wheelbarrow. "Did you come to help me clean out the sheep pen?"

"May I?" Edward asked eagerly.

"Let me see. I think there is a shovel around here that I used when I was just a little bigger than you," Roger answered. "Just wait here. I'll see if I can find it."

Roger disappeared around the corner into another part of the barn. Soon he returned. "I found it!" He handed the shovel to Edward. "Now we can work together. This shouldn't take long with four hands to do it."

When they were finished, Roger said, "I don't have anything else that I need to do right away. How would you like to take a ride on Midget, our pet pony?"

Edward's eyes shone. "I would like that!"

Roger led the way to the pasture, where the pony was grazing. He whistled to Midget, and she came trotting to him. Roger lifted the boy

onto the pony's back and snapped a rope around her neck. Then he led her in and out the driveway several times with Edward on her back.

"This is fun!" Edward exclaimed. "I wish we had a pony at home."

Edward was having such a nice time that it did not seem long at all until Mother called him, ready to go home.

"Roger is such a nice boy!" Edward bubbled on the way home. "He let me ride his pony and help him clean the sheep pen. When I grow up, I want to be like Roger."

Mother smiled. "I am glad Roger likes to do things with you," she said.

That evening Edward was playing on the floor. Mother was sitting on the couch sewing buttons on a shirt, and Father was reading in his easy chair.

"Roger is so good with children," Edward heard Mother tell Father. "Edward enjoys going to Brother Virgil's to be with Roger. If only Roger would give his heart to the Lord."

Edward looked up at Mother. "Mother, what does 'give his heart to the Lord' mean?" he asked.

"When children are small, God's plan is for

them to obey their parents," Father explained. "They are happy when they obey. When they grow older, God calls them and wants them to follow Him. He wants them to become Christians."

"Isn't Roger a Christian?" Edward asked.

"No, he isn't," Mother said sadly.

Edward was quiet as he went back to his play. "I want Roger to be a Christian," he thought.

When Father came to pray with Edward that night, Edward asked, "Father, may I pray that Roger will be a Christian?"

"Yes, you may," Father replied. "That will be a good thing to pray about."

Edward knelt beside Father. "Dear God," he prayed. "Thank You for Father and Mother. Thank You for our house and for our food to eat. Thank You that Roger let me ride his pony today. Help Roger to want to be a Christian. In Jesus' Name. Amen."

Then Father prayed. He prayed for Roger too. Then they got up from their knees, and Father tucked Edward into bed.

"Father, will Roger be a Christian if we pray for him?" Edward asked.

"We don't know, Edward," Father said. "But

we must keep on praying for Roger. God wants us to do that. He wants Roger to be a Christian, and so do we."

"Yes," Edward agreed. "Good night, Father."

"Good night, Edward," Father said as he snapped out the light and headed downstairs.

As the days went by, Edward often prayed for Roger. Father and Mother prayed for Roger too. But many weeks went by, and it seemed to Edward that his prayers were not being answered.

"Father, why doesn't Roger want to be a Christian?" Edward asked one evening when Father came to his room to pray with him.

"I don't know, son," Father answered. "Satan tries to make people believe that they will be happier if they can do things their own way instead of what God wants them to do. But that is not true at all. God's way is always best."

"But why do we keep on praying for Roger if he doesn't become a Christian anyway?" Edward asked.

"God tells us in His Word that He wants us to keep on praying even when it seems our prayers aren't answered," Father explained. "Jesus loves Roger very much. We love him too, and we want him to become a Christian. That is why we keep praying for him."

"I love Roger, and I won't stop praying for him," Edward decided.

One sunshiny morning several weeks later, Edward tripped happily down the stairs. He could smell that Mother was making pancakes, and pancakes were his favorite breakfast.

"Good morning, Edward," Mother greeted him with a smile. "God gave us a lovely day, didn't He?"

Edward nodded as he went to the sink to wash his hands. "I'm going to play in the sandbox after I've dried the dishes," he said.

"I have some happy news for you, Edward," Mother said as she carried the plate of hot pancakes to the table.

"What is it?" Edward looked eagerly at Mother. He could tell by her shining eyes that the news was something very special.

"Sister Rhoda called this morning," Mother told him. "She said that Roger became a Christian last night."

Edward's eyes shone too. "Oh, I'm so glad!" he said. "We prayed for a long time, and now God answered our prayers, didn't He, Mother?"

"Yes, He surely did." Father had stepped into the kitchen in time to hear the last part of the conversation. Edward looked up at Father. "We should thank God for answering our prayers, shouldn't we?" he asked.

"Yes, we should," Father agreed. "Let's sit down to eat. Do you want to pray, Edward?"

Edward nodded. When they were seated, he prayed, "Dear God, thank You that Roger became a Christian. Thank You that You answered our prayers. Help me to obey You by being obedient to Father and Mother. Thank You for this food. In Jesus' Name. Amen."

12.

David's Questions

"Mother, what can I do?" David asked as he came and stood beside Mother, who was sewing buttons on one of his new shirts.

Mother thought for a moment. "Why don't you sit here at the table and color a picture in your farm coloring book?"

"Okay," David agreed readily. He went over to Father's desk. The bottom desk drawer was where Mother put David's coloring books and the paper he was allowed to use. David took out his farm coloring book and the crayons and carried them over to the table.

David sat down and opened his coloring book. "Shall I color this picture of the mother hen and her chicks?" he asked, holding the book up so that Mother could see.

"That will be fine," Mother answered.

"Mother, what color shall I make these baby chicks?" David asked as he studied the picture.

"Many chicks are yellow," Mother replied.

"Oh, yes." David reached for his yellow crayon.

David was quiet for a few moments as he colored the chicks. Then he asked, "Mother, what color shall I make the grass?"

"Grass is green, David," Mother said patiently. She reached for another button to sew onto the shirt she was finishing.

"Is that shirt for me, Mother?" David asked.

"Yes, it is," Mother replied. "It is a school shirt for you."

"Oh, good!" David clapped his hands. "How many days till school starts?"

"How many days is it, David?" Mother asked.

David ran over to the calendar beside the refrigerator. On that calendar Mother had put a red circle around the day school would start.

Every evening David put a red *X* on the day that had just passed.

"One, two, three, four, five, six . . . Six more days till school starts!" David exclaimed joyfully.

"Oh, look, David, there goes the mailman," Mother said. "Let's go and get the mail."

When they arrived at the mailbox, David opened it and pulled out the mail. "A package!" he exclaimed. "Who is the package for, Mother?"

Mother looked at the name. "It's for Father," she replied.

"Who is it from? What's in it? Why is Father getting a package?" David asked without giving Mother time to answer.

"It's from Grandmother," Mother answered. "It's probably for Father's birthday. I don't know what is in it. We will have to wait and see when Father comes home."

When they got to the house, Mother set Father's package on top of the refrigerator.

"Mother, why does Father have to go to work every day?" David asked.

"David, can you tell *me* why Father has to go to work?" Mother asked kindly. "Do you remember when Father explained that to you several days ago?"

David's eyes lighted up. "Yes, I remember," he answered. "Father told me that God wants fathers to work to earn money to buy food and clothes and other things that their families need."

"That is right," Mother approved. "David, it is good for you to ask Father and Mother questions about things you do not understand. That is the way God wants children to do. Many of your questions are good, but sometimes you already know the answers. Do you remember when you asked me what color the grass is?"

David nodded slowly.

"You knew what color grass is," Mother continued. "You have seen grass many, many times. And if you forgot, how could you find out?"

"I could look out the window at the grass," David replied.

"That's right," Mother answered. "When you go to school, Sister Rosetta will have eighteen children to help with their lessons. If each child would ask her five questions one morning, she would have ninety questions to answer. That is this many." Mother showed David by opening and closing her hands nine times.

David's eyes grew big. "That is a lot!" he exclaimed.

"Yes, it is," Mother agreed. "Father and I want to help you with things you need to learn. But we also want to help you learn to figure things out yourself when you can. That is a part of growing up."

That afternoon David was working in his preschool book. Mother had told him that the directions said he should match the animal to the food it eats. David looked at the squirrel.

"Mother," he began, "what does a—" Suddenly he stopped. He remembered what Mother had said. He would try to figure it out first. He looked at all the pictures. At the very bottom was a picture of a nut. David remembered a story Grandmother had read to him one time. In the story, the squirrel had been gathering nuts for winter. "Squirrels eat nuts!" he exclaimed out loud.

"That's right!" Mother praised him. "How did you figure it out?"

"I looked at all the pictures first," David explained. "Then when I saw the nut, I remembered the story in Grandmother's book about a squirrel. The squirrel was putting nuts into his hole to eat in the wintertime."

"Very good," Mother said. "Now I know my boy is growing up. Remember, Father and I want you to ask questions when you do not know something. But sometimes we have given you an answer that you could have remembered if you had thought about it, like this time. The story you remembered in Grandmother's book helped to answer your question. See if you can do that more often," Mother encouraged.

"I will try," David promised as he bent his head over his workbook again.

13.

Ruth and the Bear Book

"Good morning, Ruth," Mother greeted as Ruth came into the kitchen.

"Good morning," Ruth returned cheerfully as she went to the sink to wash her hands.

Mother flipped over another pancake on the griddle. "Do you know what, Ruth? Meredith's mother called this morning and wondered if we could keep Meredith for a few hours while she goes to the doctor."

"Oh, good!" Ruth clapped her hands. "I like it when little children come to our house. I wish

I would have a little brother or sister to play with every day."

"I know you enjoy little children," Mother answered with a smile. "And so do I. God is pleased when girls enjoy little children. God made you that way because someday He may want you to be a mother with little children. Or you might be a schoolteacher who teaches other people's children.

"We would be happy if God gave us another baby, but we know that God's will is best. Someone has to be the youngest in the family, you know."

"Yes, I know," Ruth answered. "And I want to be happy with God's will. I will just enjoy the little children who come to our house."

"Good," Mother answered. "And so will I."

Soon after breakfast a gray car drove in the lane. Meredith and her mother got out and walked to the house. Meredith was holding tightly to her mother's hand.

Meredith's mother talked to Ruth's mother for a few minutes; then she left. Meredith stood looking out the window, and her eyes filled with tears.

"Why don't you take Meredith to the living room and play with her," Mother suggested.

"Then I think she will be happy."

"Come, Meredith, shall we play with toys?" Ruth asked.

Meredith's eyes lit up. "Yes, let's play with toys," she said.

When Mother came into the living room a few minutes later, Ruth was sitting on the floor, building a block tower for Meredith.

Crash! Meredith pushed the tower over. She looked at Ruth and giggled.

"Shall we build it again?" Ruth asked.

"Build it again," Meredith said.

"Ruth," Mother said, "I need to hang out the next load of wash. Do you think you can keep Meredith happy while I do that?"

"I think so," Ruth answered. "We're having fun, aren't we, Meredith?"

"We're having fun," Meredith said, smiling at Mother.

Mother went to the laundry room and took the clothes out of the washer. Soon Ruth heard the kitchen door open and close as Mother went outside.

Meredith went over to the bag her mother had brought along for her. She pulled out a book. "Read this," she begged.

Ruth took the book. "Come. Let's sit on the

couch," she said. "Then I'll read to you." Ruth went over to the couch and sat down, and Meredith climbed up beside her.

"'Far away in a land called Bear Country, there lived four bears,'" Ruth began. "'Father Bear, Mother Bear, Brother Bear, and Sister Bear lived in a cozy little tree house at the edge of Grizzlyville.'" Ruth read several more pages. The story told about Brother Bear and Sister Bear's bad manners. Father Bear thought that he and Mother Bear should not mind it because all cubs acted that way, but Mother Bear thought it was time to teach them a lesson. So she made a chart, and each time someone forgot to mind his manners, he had to do an extra job for Mother Bear.

The kitchen door opened and closed again, and Mother came into the living room. She stood for a moment listening to the story. "What book are you reading, Ruth?" she asked.

Ruth held up the book. "This one," she answered. "Meredith got it out of her bag."

"Put the book back in the bag now," Mother said. "I'm ready to go for milk. Do you girls want to go with me?"

"Yes, yes!" Ruth answered. The Millers' farm,

where Ruth's family got their milk, was just a half mile down the road. Ruth often walked with Mother to get the milk.

"I go too?" Meredith asked, looking up at Mother.

"Yes, you will go too," Mother answered. "Ruth, will you bring the jar please?"

Ruth picked up the empty milk jar from the table. Mother went to get her wallet.

"Mother, Meredith could ride in the wagon," Ruth suggested.

"Yes, that would be a good idea," Mother agreed. "She would enjoy that. Here, let me take the milk jar while you bring the wagon."

Meredith squealed happily as Ruth pulled the wagon up to the porch. "Me have a ride," she said.

"Yes, you will have a ride." Mother swung Meredith into the wagon and set the milk jar in one corner. Then they started on their way with Ruth pulling the wagon and Mother walking along beside it.

"Well, it looks like you have an extra girl today," Sister Harmony said when they arrived at the Millers' house. "This is Meredith, isn't it?" She chucked the little girl under the chin and gave her a friendly smile.

"Yes," Mother answered. "Her mother went to the doctor and left Meredith at our house."

"It's almost like having a little sister," Ruth said. "Only I wish she'd stay all the time."

Sister Harmony smiled. "But at least you can enjoy her today," she said. "That's special, isn't it?"

Ruth nodded and smiled.

Soon Ruth, Meredith, and Mother started for home again. Just as they reached the house, Meredith's mother drove in the lane. She talked to Mother a little bit, and then she and Meredith went home.

"Mother, that book about the bears was interesting," Ruth said. "I wish I could have finished it."

"I didn't want you to finish that book, Ruth," Mother answered.

"Why, Mother?" Ruth asked. "It's not a bad book, is it? Mother Bear was teaching the little bears good manners. That was good, wasn't it? You teach me to be polite too."

"Yes, I know," Mother answered. "There are some good things about that book, but it does not teach good manners the way God planned that children should be taught. The Bible tells us that people are living souls. They will live on forever, even after their bodies die. But animals will not live forever. They just go back to the earth when they die.

"Some people do not want to think about having a soul. They do not want to obey God, and they do not want to believe that wicked people will go to hell when they die. They try to believe that people are just like animals. Christians know that God has a special plan for people, and they know we should not try to make animals act like people."

Ruth frowned. She was trying hard to understand. "Animals can't think and talk like people do, can they?"

"No," Mother answered. "And I don't believe God is pleased with stories that make animals act like people. God didn't write the Bible that way, and Christians follow God's example in the way they write and talk.

"Also," Mother continued, "in that book Father Bear acts almost as naughty as the cubs. Mother Bear has to scold him too. That isn't God's plan either. God planned for fathers to be leaders in the home and to help the family to obey God."

"It sounds like it is not a good book to read after all," Ruth decided.

"Good," Mother approved. "The Bible and other stories written by Christian people teach us how to obey God. They are the kind of books we want to read because they please God."

14.

Was James Awake?

"That was a good lunch, Mother," four-year-old Crystal said, patting her stomach. "Especially the cheese sandwiches."

"Thank you," Mother said, smiling at Crystal. "I am glad you enjoyed it. Now I need to wash the dishes, and I need a helper to dry them for me."

"I will!" Crystal said. She ran to the closet to get her stool.

There were not many lunch dishes, and it did not take long at all to wash them.

"Now what are you going to do?" Crystal asked as Mother hung up her dishcloth and Crystal's tea towel.

"I am going to feed James and put him to bed for his nap," Mother answered. "Then I want to go out and hoe the corn."

"May I go outside with you?" Crystal asked eagerly.

"Yes, you may," Mother answered. She carried James over to the rocking chair and sat down to feed him. After a while he fell asleep, and Mother took him to the bedroom.

"Are you ready to go outside now?" Crystal asked when Mother came out of the bedroom.

"Yes," Mother answered. Together they walked out into the warm sunshine. It was a lovely afternoon with a cool breeze blowing.

"I'll get the hoe for you," Crystal offered. She quickly ran to the garage and soon returned with the hoe.

Mother began hoeing, and Crystal walked over to the sandbox. She built a bridge and a little house and a store. Then she made roads with the shovel.

"It would be more fun if James was playing with me," she thought. "Even if he sometimes wrecks my roads and other things that I make, I still like it when he plays with me."

After a while Crystal asked, "Mother, how soon will James wake up?"

"Oh, I hope he sleeps at least another hour," Mother answered. "If he wakes up too soon, he gets grouchy before bedtime."

Slowly Crystal drove her little toy car from her house to the store. Then she pretended to buy bread and soap and eggs. Then she drove back home again.

"Crystal," Mother said when she reached the end of her fourth row, "maybe you should go and check on James. If he would wake up, we couldn't hear him cry from out here. Just open the door softly and peek in. If he is crying, come and call me."

Crystal jumped up and brushed the sand from her dress. She skipped lightly to the house and opened the door. "I hope James is awake," she thought. "I'm tired of playing alone."

Crystal peeked in the door. James was lying in his crib. His eyes were closed, and his little hand lay against his cheek. He looked so sweet and dear.

Crystal was disappointed. "I wish he would

wake up," she thought. "Maybe if I would say his name, he would open his eyes."

"James," she whispered. "James, do you want to wake up?"

James opened his eyes and rubbed them sleepily. When he saw his big sister, he reached out his chubby arms.

"I can't get you by myself, James," Crystal told him. "I must call Mother."

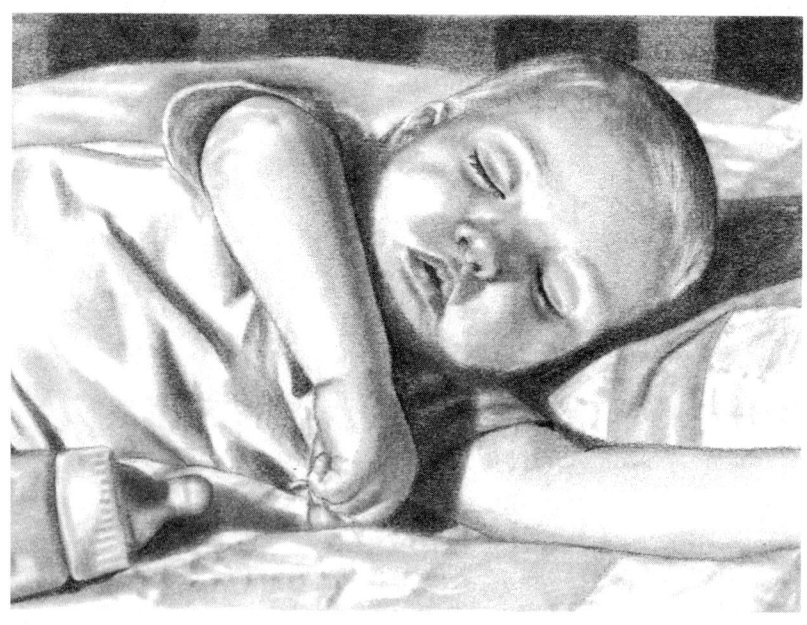

Crystal hurried outside. But she did not feel happy. She knew she had disobeyed Mother.

"Mother!" she called. "James is awake."

Mother laid down her hoe and came into the house. "Was he crying when you looked into the bedroom?" she asked Crystal.

Crystal looked down at the floor. She did not answer Mother's question.

"Crystal, did you wake James?" Mother asked, lifting Crystal's chin and looking into her eyes.

Tears welled up in Crystal's eyes. Slowly she nodded her head.

"Ma-ma, Ma-ma," James cried.

"I must get James and change his diaper. But then I will need to punish you, Crystal, for disobeying me," Mother said.

After Mother had taken care of James, she said, "Come with me, Crystal."

Tears filled Crystal's eyes again as she followed Mother to the bedroom. She knew she deserved to be punished because she had not obeyed her mother.

Mother spanked Crystal; then she took her on her lap.

"Crystal," she explained, "Father and I must punish you when you disobey so that you learn not to take your own way. If we do not do it when you are young, you will find it very hard to obey God when you grow up."

"I'm sorry, Mother," Crystal said when she had stopped crying. "I wanted James to wake up so that I could play with him, but I'm sorry that I disobeyed."

"I am glad you are sorry. Disobedience never makes us happy," Mother said. "The Bible says to children, 'Keep thy father's commandment, and forsake not the law of thy mother.' A commandment is something that you are told to do. Mother knew that James should have a longer nap. But you did not think about making Mother or James happy. You only thought about what you wanted. But disobeying did not make you happy either, did it Crystal?"

Crystal shook her head. "I will try to obey after this," she promised.

"That is good," Mother said with a smile as Crystal slid from her lap. "Now let's all go outside. I want to finish hoeing the corn."

Mother carried James outside.

"May James play in the sandbox with me?" Crystal asked.

"Yes, but you must watch him closely to make sure he doesn't put sand in his mouth,"

Mother answered. Mother placed James in the sandbox and gave him some toys.

Crystal sat down in the sandbox too. She liked very much to play with James, but disobeying had not made her happy at all.

15.

The Birthday Blackboard

"Evelyn! Dorcas!" Mother called. "It's time to get up!"

Evelyn slowly turned over and rubbed her sleepy eyes. Dorcas sat up beside her.

"Today is my birthday," Dorcas announced happily. "And Grandpa and Grandma are coming for dinner!"

"Oh, yes!" Now Evelyn was wide awake too. The two girls hopped out of bed and began to get dressed.

"Mother, when are Grandpa and Grandma

coming?" Evelyn asked as they entered the kitchen.

"They will come just before dinner," Mother answered. "I could use two helpers this morning to help me get ready."

"We'll help," Dorcas and Evelyn said together.

The two girls were very busy that morning. First Dorcas washed the dishes and Evelyn dried them. Then Dorcas swept the floor, and Evelyn dusted the furniture in the living room. After that Dorcas played with baby Elson to keep him happy while Evelyn helped Mother set the table for dinner.

Dorcas went to the window with Elson. "Do you want to look out the window?" she asked him. "Maybe we can see Grandpa's coming soon."

Elson put his little hands on the window and cooed happily. He pointed to Tabby, who was walking across the yard.

"Do you see the kitty?" Dorcas asked him.

A blue car turned in the lane. "They're here! They're here!" Dorcas called.

Evelyn came hurrying to the window. "Oh, good!" she exclaimed happily. She hurried out to meet Grandpa and Grandma, and Dorcas followed with Elson. Mother came too.

"Mother, will you take Elson, please?" Dorcas asked.

Mother took the baby from Dorcas's arms. Dorcas quickly ran to join Evelyn at the end of the walk.

"Well, well, how are our two girls?" Grandma asked. She gave Evelyn and Dorcas each a hug.

"Fine," they giggled.

Evelyn saw that Dorcas was looking at the package that Grandpa was carrying under his arm. "I wish it was my birthday," Evelyn thought. "Then it would be my present."

"And here is something for the birthday girl," Grandpa said, handing the package to Dorcas.

"Thank you! May I open it now?" Dorcas asked.

"Why don't you wait until we are at the table," Grandpa suggested. "Father and Leon would probably like to watch you open it too."

"Okay," Dorcas agreed. She shook the package and listened for a sound, but she could not hear anything. Then she felt it. "It's soft on one side, like a pillow, but it's hard on the other side. Whatever can it be?"

Evelyn felt it too, but she could not figure

it out either. She could hardly wait till dinner-time.

Finally dinner was ready. Mother called everyone to the table. After Grandpa had led in prayer, Dorcas picked up her package and began to unwrap it.

"Oh, it's a blackboard and a box of chalk!" she exclaimed, pulling them out of the wrapping paper. "But why is the blackboard soft on one side?"

"That is so you can put it on your lap while you are writing," Grandma explained.

"Oh, I understand now." Dorcas put the blackboard on her lap. She pulled a piece of chalk out of the box and began to write. "This is nice. Thank you, Grandpa and Grandma."

"You're welcome," Grandpa and Grandma answered.

"All right. Now put the blackboard away and wash your hands," Mother instructed. "It's time to eat. After dinner you can write on it some more."

Dorcas obediently took the blackboard and laid it on the counter. She washed her hands and returned to the table.

"Dorcas, I want you to clear the plates and the glasses off the table," Mother said when dinner was over. "Evelyn, you do the silverware. Grandma and I will wash and dry the dishes this time."

"Good!" the girls cheered. The jobs Mother had given them did not seem like big jobs at all. Often they had to wash and dry the dishes.

Soon Evelyn was finished. She picked up Dorcas's blackboard and carried it over to the sofa. Taking a blue piece of chalk from the box, she began to carefully write her name.

When Dorcas was finished with her job, she came over to Evelyn. "May I have it now, please?" she asked.

Evelyn pulled the board away from her sister. "I had it first."

"But it's mine, and I have hardly written on it yet," Dorcas said.

"No." Evelyn began to write again.

"Mother." Dorcas walked across the kitchen to stand beside Mother, who was drying the dishes. "Evelyn has my blackboard, and she won't let me have it."

Mother looked over at Evelyn. "Evelyn, let Dorcas write on her blackboard now. It is hers."

"But she has to share," Evelyn objected. "I had it first."

"She will share with you later," Mother said. "But you must let her have it now. How would you like it if it was your birthday present and she would use it first?"

Evelyn thought about that. "I guess I wouldn't like it," she said slowly. "Here, Dorcas. You may have your blackboard."

"Thank you," Dorcas said.

"Mother, may I have a piece of paper to draw on?" Evelyn asked.

"Yes, you may," Mother answered. "You may get one out of the drawer."

Evelyn skipped to the desk and got a piece of paper and a pencil. She sat down at the table to draw.

"Do you know what, Evelyn?" Dorcas said. "I think we could both draw on this. Come here."

Evelyn laid down her pencil and went over to Dorcas.

Dorcas sat sideways on the sofa and crossed her legs. "Now you sit like this too," she instructed. Evelyn did as Dorcas told her to. "Now we'll put the board between us, like this. You can draw on this half, and I will draw on the other half."

The two girls giggled as they shifted around

to make themselves comfortable. Then they both began to draw.

"Well, now look at that," Grandpa said as he came out to the kitchen. "You found a good way to share your birthday present, didn't you, Dorcas?"

Dorcas smiled shyly at Grandpa.

"It's more fun when you share, isn't it?" Grandpa asked.

Dorcas nodded.

"I'm glad you have learned that lesson," Grandpa said. "People who share are always happiest."

When Grandpa walked away, Evelyn whispered to Dorcas, "Thank you for sharing your blackboard. I'm sorry I didn't let you have it at first."

"I forgive you," Dorcas said with a smile. "It's just like Grandpa said. It's more fun when we share."

16.

The Book in the Bushes

"What shall we play?" six-year-old Carolyn asked her cousins Marilyn and Lois. Sunday dinner was over, and the three girls were sitting on the porch swing.

"Let's play hide-and-seek," Marilyn suggested. "Maybe the boys will help us."

"Okay," Carolyn agreed. "Wilmer! Raymond!" she called to the boys, who were playing with Rover in the yard. "Will you help us play hide-and-seek?"

Raymond looked at Wilmer. "What do you

say? Shall we?" he asked.

"Sure," Wilmer answered. "Here, Rover. You may come too." Rover wagged his tail and followed Wilmer to the porch.

"I'll be it," Raymond offered.

"Okay," the girls agreed.

Raymond put his head against the tree trunk. "One, two, three, go!" he called. Then he began counting. "One, two, three, four, five, six, seven . . ."

The other children scattered in all directions. Carolyn hurried around the corner of the house and looked about quickly for a place to hide. Her eyes rested on the row of bushes that lined two sides of the yard. She ran over to them. Parting two of the bushes, she squatted down between them. "Good. I can see the base from here," she thought as she peered through the prickly branches in front of her.

"Ready or not, here I come!" Raymond called.

Just then Carolyn heard voices behind her. She turned to look. Two boys on bicycles were coming around the curve in the road. They were talking to each other.

Soon the boys were riding past the row of

bushes. Carolyn watched them. Then she saw one of them toss something into the bushes.

"What was that?" she wondered. "It looks like a book."

"Free!" Carolyn heard Lois holler. Lois had arrived at the base. Raymond came running, but he was too late.

For a short time Raymond stood near the base, carefully guarding it. But soon he walked slowly to the corner of the house and disappeared.

Carolyn bent low till she was around the bushes; then she made a dash for the base. "Free!" she called.

Raymond had come around the corner again in time to see her coming. He ran too, but he was too late. "Ah!" he exclaimed. "I'll have to watch better."

They played for about half an hour. Then Carolyn said, "I'm getting hot. Let's stop playing."

"Okay," the others agreed.

"Let's go see the new calf," Raymond suggested to Wilmer. Wilmer agreed, and the boys headed toward the barn.

"Come with me," Carolyn said to Lois and Marilyn. "I want to see something."

"What do you want to see?" Marilyn asked curiously.

"When I was hiding in the bushes, two boys rode by on bicycles," Carolyn answered. "One of them threw something into the bushes. I want to see what it is. I think it's a book."

Carolyn walked over to the spot where she had seen it land. Reaching under the bushes, she drew out a small book.

"It *is* a book," she said. "That's what I thought. Let's sit here and look at it." The two other girls sat down on each side of Carolyn. Carolyn opened the book.

"Oh, those pictures are not nice!" Marilyn exclaimed. "I think they are bad pictures. Maybe we should show the book to your mother."

"I'm going to," Carolyn answered. "But I want to look at it first."

"What are you girls looking at?" A voice above the girls startled them. They looked up and saw Aunt Marie standing there.

"A—a book," Carolyn answered.

"What book is it? May I see it?" Aunt Marie asked.

Slowly Carolyn handed the book to Aunt Marie.

Aunt Marie glanced at a page or two in the

book, then closed it. She looked at the girls. "Where did you find this book?" she asked.

"Here in the bushes." Carolyn pointed. "We were playing hide-and-seek. I was hiding here in the bushes, and I saw two boys on bicycles

riding past. One of them threw this book into the bushes."

"Such a book needs to be burned," Aunt Marie said. "It is not a good book for you or anyone to look at. Perhaps those boys don't have godly parents to help them to fill their minds with good things.

"Books like this are like poison to our minds. When we look at such pictures, it is very hard to forget them. God can help us forget, but it is much, much better to never look at them. These pictures were made by people who are serving Satan, not God. We want to fill our minds with things that please God."

The girls listened very soberly.

"David said in Psalm 101:3, 'I will set no wicked thing before mine eyes.' We need to decide like David did that we will not look at wicked things."

"I'm sorry for looking at the book, Aunt Marie," Carolyn said.

"I'm sorry too," Marilyn and Lois added.

"I'm glad you are sorry," Aunt Marie said. "Now, if you ever find such a book again, what should you do?"

"Give it to Father or Mother right away," Lois said quietly.

"That is right," Aunt Marie said. "Always remember that. There is a verse in the Bible that tells us to think about things that are pure and lovely and true. We should think about how to obey and praise God. If you learn to do that when you are young, you will save yourselves much trouble when you are older.

"And now," Aunt Marie said, smiling at the girls, "let's get rid of this book. Then, if you would like, I can read you some stories from a good book that will please God."

"Yes, yes! Please do, Aunt Marie," Marilyn said.

"Yes," the other girls agreed.

"I will get *Across the Rose Hedge With Aunt Merry*," Carolyn suggested. "Mother has been reading it to me at bedtime. I'll ask her if you may read it to us."

Soon Marilyn and Lois were seated beside Aunt Marie on the porch swing, and Carolyn on a footstool at her feet.

"I am glad we are going to read a book that pleases God," Carolyn said. "I knew I should give the other book to Mother, but I wanted to look at it first. But if I find a book like that again, I will give it to her right away."

"Good," Aunt Marie approved as she opened

Across the Rose Hedge With Aunt Merry. "If you do that, you will be learning to make right choices. You will be pleasing God and your parents like the Bible says."

17.

Chicken Pox Lesson

"Oh, I stepped on my shoestring!" eight-year-old Kendall exclaimed as he opened the school-house door. He placed his lunch box on the shelf in the coatroom and bent down to tie his shoe.

"So you're here this morning?" Kendall's friend Elvin stuck his head around the door-way. "I thought maybe you would have chicken pox too."

Kendall looked puzzled. "Why did you think I might have chicken pox?"

"Didn't you find out?" Elvin asked. "Jane and Allen have chicken pox! They won't be coming to school today."

"Oh," Kendall said. "How do you feel when you have chicken pox?" He had heard people talking about chicken pox already, but he had never seen someone who had them.

"Mother said you get little spots on your skin. Often they itch terribly," Elvin told him. "And you might have a fever. And if you get close to someone who has chicken pox, you might get them too."

"Oh, I hope I don't get them," Kendall said.

"I don't want to get them either," Elvin said. "I hate being sick."

That evening after school Kendall burst into the house. "Do you know what, Mother?" he exclaimed excitedly as he set his lunch box on the table.

"No. What?" Mother asked, looking up from her sewing.

"The Miller children have chicken pox! Jane and Allen were both missing from school today."

"I see," Mother said. "I suppose that means it will be going around at school."

"Do you think we'll get them?" Kendall asked worriedly.

"You and Rachel haven't had them yet, so I won't be surprised if you do," Mother answered. "Brenda and Jeremy had them when Brenda was in first grade. Usually someone who had them once won't get them again."

"I remember when Jeremy and I had them," fifteen-year-old Brenda said. She and Rachel had entered the house while Mother and Kendall were talking. "I remember that they were really itchy, but Mother said we must not scratch them because they might become infected or leave scars. Mother read stories and sang to us to try to help us forget how miserable we were. And Father bought us each a grape soda for a special treat!"

"I don't want to get chicken pox even if I do get a grape soda!" Kendall stated emphatically.

"Neither do I," Rachel added.

"Let's not worry about it," Mother said. "Worrying won't help. Lots of other children have had chicken pox, and they got over them." She smiled at the children. "Now, you may each have an apple from the pantry. Then go change your clothes and do your chores. We have prayer meeting this evening."

That evening after prayer meeting, Kendall whispered to Elvin, "Let's stay away from

everybody. Mother says the chicken pox will probably go around, and we might get them. I don't want to get chicken pox. If we stay away from the other children, maybe we won't get them."

"All right," Elvin agreed. "Let's. I surely don't want to get them either."

"Hello, Kendall and Elvin," Merlin greeted them cheerily.

"Hello," they replied. But as soon as they could, they slipped away from Merlin. Merlin looked puzzled, but he soon went to find someone else to talk to.

"Here comes Ray," Elvin whispered. "Let's go away before he sees us."

"If we stand behind Brother Paul and Brother Philip, Ray won't be able to see us," Kendall suggested.

The two boys stayed together all evening. Whenever any of the other children came close, they tried to slip away from them.

"Mother, Elvin and I stayed away from all the other children this evening," Kendall announced when the family was on their way home from prayer meeting.

"You stayed away from them? What do you mean?" Mother asked.

"We don't want to get chicken pox," Kendall explained. "So we stayed away from the other children."

"You weren't unkind to anyone, were you?" Father asked, looking at Kendall.

"Oh, no," Kendall said quickly. "We weren't unkind. We just tried not to let them see us, and if they came close, we walked away."

"Why are you so scared of chicken pox?" Brenda asked.

"Well, you said that when you had them, they were really itchy and you weren't even allowed to scratch them," Kendall said. "I don't want to be itchy. And besides, I don't want to miss school."

The next afternoon after school the children brought more news to Mother.

"Oh, Mother, guess what!" Brenda exclaimed. She looked at Kendall and smiled. "You know how Kendall and Elvin tried to stay away from the other children last evening so that they wouldn't get chicken pox? Well, now Elvin has them!"

Mother smiled. "Well, I guess it didn't do a lot of good for you to try to stay away from the others, did it?" she asked Kendall.

Kendall shook his head sheepishly.

"That is the way it often is," Mother said. "It is all right not to go places where people have a sickness that we could get from them, if it isn't necessary. But often we can't help it. And it is always wrong to be unkind or impolite to people who we think might give us a sickness, or for any other reason. God wants us to be kind to everyone."

Kendall nodded slowly. "I still don't want to get chicken pox," he said. "But I guess I won't try so hard again. It didn't work very well anyway."

"If you get sick, I will take care of you as I did Brenda and Jeremy," Mother said. "You may be miserable for a while, but you will get better. God will help you to be brave just as He has helped you other times when you were sick or had hard things to do. When you feel worried about getting chicken pox, try to remember those things. That will help you not to worry so much."

"I will try," Kendall promised.

"In devotions this morning at school, Sister Ruth read the verse 'Let not your heart be troubled, neither let it be afraid,'" Brenda added. "Isn't that a good verse to remember when we are worried about something, Mother?"

"Yes, it is," Mother agreed. "Many times we face things that we can't do anything about. We don't know if Kendall will get chicken pox or not. But we won't try so hard to stay away from them that we can't be friendly or happy." She smiled at Kendall. "We want to trust God and remember that His will is best for us."

Kendall nodded as he started for the stairs to change his clothes.

18.

The Wrong Thing to Talk About

Sunday school was over, and seven-year-old Landon slipped into his seat beside Father. Father looked down and smiled at Landon, and Landon smiled back. Then he joined in as the congregation began to sing, "'I must tell Jesus all of my trials; / I cannot bear these burdens alone . . .'"

Landon looked over to the women's side. He could see Mother sitting next to the center aisle with baby Martha on her lap. Five-year-old Abbie was sitting beside her. Landon saw

Mother lean over and whisper something to Abbie. Then Mother got up and went down the aisle to the mothers' room with Martha.

Landon looked down at the song book he was sharing with Father. But soon he looked up at Father. Father was looking over to where Abbie was sitting. Landon looked too. He saw that Abbie was giggling and whispering to her friend Nancy, who was sitting beside her.

"Abbie is being naughty," Landon thought. "She thinks that Mother can't see her, but she doesn't know that Father is watching her. She will probably be punished when we get home."

Just then Landon saw Sister Wendy reach over and pull Abbie toward her. Sister Wendy leaned over and whispered something to Abbie. Abbie looked soberly up at Sister Wendy. She sat quietly. She did not whisper and giggle anymore.

When church was over, Landon visited for a while with his friend David. Soon Father touched his shoulder. "Come, Landon," Father said. "Martha is very fussy this morning, and Mother is ready to go home."

Landon said good-bye to David and followed Father out to the car. Soon the Risser family was on their way home.

"I saw something this morning that I didn't like to see," Father said, looking in the rearview mirror at Abbie. Abbie squirmed and looked down at her lap.

"You know that Mother and I do not want you to giggle and whisper to your friends during church," Father continued. "When Mother goes out to the mothers' room with Martha, she trusts you to behave. I'm glad that Sister Wendy told you to be quiet. But I am going to have to punish you when we get home."

Landon looked at his sister. Abbie's eyes were filling with tears. "I'm glad I was good in church," he thought. "Abbie is probably going to get a spanking."

When they arrived home, Father and Abbie went to the study.

"Landon, set the table please," Mother requested. "Set an extra place because Sister Amy is coming for dinner."

Landon hummed to himself as he carefully carried the plates to the table. Soon Abbie came out to the kitchen. Her eyes were red from crying, but she smiled at Landon. "May I help you set the table?" she asked.

"You may give everyone a spoon," Landon answered. He opened the drawer and got out the knives, forks, and spoons. He handed the spoons to Abbie.

"Abbie, did Father spank you?" Landon asked in a low voice as they carried the silverware to the table.

Abbie looked down at the floor and did not answer.

"What did you say, Landon?" Mother asked as she opened the drawer to get the bread knife.

Now it was Landon's turn to look at the floor. "I—I—I—" he stammered.

"Did you ask Abbie if she got a spanking?" Mother asked.

Landon nodded his head slowly.

"That is none of your business, Landon," Mother said firmly. "I do not want you to ask that question again. Do you understand?"

Landon nodded again.

"Sister Amy is here!" Abbie called. "Shall I tell her to come in, Mother?"

"Yes, you may," Mother answered.

After the dinner dishes were done, Mother went to put Martha to bed. "Shall I read the *Wee Lambs* to you?" Sister Amy asked Landon and Abbie.

"Yes, yes!" Abbie's eyes shone. "I'll go and get it."

"Do you know what, Sister Amy?" Landon said. "Abbie was naughty in church this morning. She was whispering to Katie, and she wasn't sitting still. Father took her to the study when we got home. I think she got a spanking, but Mother said I'm not supposed to ask her about it."

"I see," Sister Amy said. "God wants us to be reverent in His house. Your parents want to help you learn that."

Abbie returned to the kitchen with the *Wee Lambs*, and Mother came right behind her. Mother sat down at the table. Abbie and Landon pulled up chairs beside Sister Amy.

When Sister Amy was finished reading the *Wee Lambs,* she and Mother visited for a while. Then Sister Amy left.

That evening Grandmother and Grandfather stopped in for a visit. Father was still in the barn when they arrived, so Grandfather decided to go out too.

"I'll go with you," Landon said, running for his boots.

"I think Abbie got a spanking today," Landon told Grandfather as they entered the barn. "She was naughty in church."

"I see," Grandfather said.

Father was in the entryway. He heard what Landon said. "Landon, I don't want to hear you talk about that anymore," he said firmly.

Landon's face got warm. He looked soberly at Father.

"Shall we look at the calves?" Grandfather suggested. "How is your calf, Pansy, doing?"

"Oh, she is growing fast!" Landon forgot his embarrassment as he led Grandfather to the calf pens.

Later that evening, when Grandfather and Grandmother had left, Father called Landon into the study.

"Landon," Father began after he had shut the door, "I am disappointed to hear you talking so much about the punishment Abbie got today. For one thing, Abbie's disobedience and her punishment are for Mother and me to take care of. It is not your business. The Bible also tells us, 'Be ye kind one to another, tender-hearted, *forgiving one another.'* Abbie is sorry that she did wrong, and I told her that she is forgiven. You need to forgive her too, and if you forgive her, you won't keep on talking about it. You get spankings too. How would you like it if, when you got a spanking, Abbie would tell others about it?"

Landon thought about that. "I wouldn't like it," he said quietly.

"No, you wouldn't," Father agreed. "There are many things that happen in our family that are all right to tell others. But there are some things that should be kept private in a family. Mother and I want to help you learn which things are all right for you to tell others. When someone gets a spanking, that is not something for you to share with others. If I hear you doing it again, I will need to punish you. Do you understand?"

Landon slowly nodded his head. "I'm sorry, Father."

"I'm glad to hear you say that," Father said kindly. "You may go now."

Landon thoughtfully left the study. "After this, I want to only say kind things about others," he decided as he headed upstairs to bed.

19.

Tell Mother About It

"Wendy, your mother is here!" Aunt Jean called.

Eight-year-old Wendy scooted down the stairs, followed by her cousins Sylvia and Kaylene. Wendy had spent the morning at Uncle Earl's house while Mother went to the dentist.

"Good-bye, Wendy," Sylvia said as Wendy followed Mother out the door.

"Good-bye, Sylvia and Kaylene," Wendy returned, turning around to wave to her cousins.

"Did you have a nice time with your cousins?" Mother asked as she started the car.

"Yes, I guess," Wendy answered. Then she stared out the window. She was thinking about something that had happened at Uncle Earl's. "I hope Mother won't ask what we played," she thought. "Kaylene told me not to tell."

Mother looked over at Wendy. She noticed that Wendy was very quiet. "Are you tired, Wendy?" she asked.

"A little," Wendy answered.

When they arrived home, Mother went to the kitchen to make a quick dinner. Wendy went to the living room and got a book from the bookcase. She sat down on the sofa to read.

"Wendy, please come and set the table," Mother called.

Wendy slowly laid down her book and walked to the kitchen. She set the table. Then she went to the basement for a jar of peaches. Soon Father came in, and the family sat down to eat.

Wendy did not really feel like eating, but she managed to finish her sandwich and a little bit of soup.

"Do you want a cookie, Wendy?" Father

asked as he held out the plate of cookies.

Wendy shook her head. "I'm full," she answered.

Father looked at her in concern. It was unusual for Wendy to refuse a cookie. "Are you sick, Wendy?" he asked.

"Not really." Wendy shook her head.

When dinner was over, Father went outside again. Wendy cleared the table while Mother began washing the dishes.

"Wendy," Mother said, "did something happen at Uncle Earl's that is bothering you? You don't seem to be your sunny self since we came home."

Wendy looked down at the silverware she was holding. Her eyes filled with tears.

"Tell Mother about it," Mother said gently. "You'll feel better." She put her arm around Wendy and waited.

"We—we played house in the hallway upstairs," Wendy told Mother. "Then Kaylene went into one of the bedrooms—the one where her big sisters, Connie and Laura, sleep. She said I should come too; she wanted to show me something. She opened some of the dresser drawers and showed me what was in them. We played with some of the things too.

"I didn't feel very good about it. I didn't think we should be playing with their things, but Kaylene said it was okay. After a while we heard Aunt Jean calling us. Then Kaylene quickly stuffed the things back in and shut the drawers. She told me not to tell you or Aunt Jean or her sisters."

Mother looked concerned. "No wonder you have been feeling bad," she said kindly. "You were not treating Kaylene's sisters kindly. And it certainly isn't good for you to be playing something that you can't tell Mother about."

Mother was quiet for several minutes. "I am very glad you told me about this, Wendy." Mother's face became sad as she continued. "When I was a girl just a little older than you are, I heard our neighbor boy saying something that was very bad. I should have talked to my mother about it, but I didn't. I kept thinking about it, and one day I told some of my friends what the boy had said. We laughed about it. I knew we shouldn't have done that, and it made me feel badly. Sometimes when I was in bed I would think about it. But I still didn't tell Mother. That made it easier for me to keep more things hidden from my father and mother.

"When children don't talk to their parents about things that trouble them, it becomes much harder for them to understand God's call when they are older. God gave you parents to help you to understand what is right and what is wrong. He also gave you a conscience. Your conscience is what makes you feel bad when you do something you shouldn't. Whenever your conscience makes you feel bad about something, be sure to come and talk to Mother or Father about it."

Wendy was listening soberly. "I will," she promised.

"I will talk to Aunt Jean about this," Mother said. "I think you girls should play downstairs or outside rather than upstairs. When you are upstairs and no one older is with you, it is easy to get into things you shouldn't. But you can forget about it now. Just remember that the next time something happens that makes you feel badly, go and tell an older person right away. If Father or I are there, you should tell us. But if you are at someone else's house and Father and I aren't there, you can tell their mother."

As Wendy picked up the milk pitcher and carried it to the refrigerator, she felt much happier. She was glad she had told Mother all about it.

Several weeks later, Wendy's family was visiting at Sister Esther's house. Sister Esther lived alone in a trailer near the church. Brother Joel's were there too. Wendy was glad because Sara and Susanna were her friends.

"May we play with your dolls?" Susanna asked Sister Esther.

"Sure," Sister Esther answered. "They are in the back room." Sister Esther led the way, and the girls followed.

"You may play in here if you leave the other things alone," Sister Esther said.

Wendy looked around. "This must also be Sister Esther's sewing room," she decided, seeing the sewing machine next to the window. Beside the sewing machine was a little desk with a typewriter on it.

The girls played with the dolls for a while. Sister Esther had pretty dolls. Wendy's doll had dark braids. She had three pretty dresses, and she even had a pacifier.

"I wonder what is in this cupboard," Sara said after a while. She pointed to a cupboard that was built into the wall above the toy chest.

"I don't know, but I don't think we should

open it," Susanna said. "Remember, Sister Esther said we should leave the other things alone."

"She won't care if I look in this one cupboard." Sara opened the cupboard door. "Oh, it's a shelf full of books!" She pulled one of the books out.

"Sara, you'd better put it back," Susanna said. But the book looked interesting, and the girls crowded around to look at it.

"Oh, look at that little girl! She has ugly red blotches all over her skin!" Sara exclaimed. "I wonder what's wrong with her."

As Sara turned a few more pages, Wendy began to feel worse and worse. She did not think they should be looking at this book.

Then Wendy remembered what Mother had said. Mother had told her that if she felt bad about something, she should come and tell her right away. Wendy stood up and headed toward the door.

"Where are you going, Wendy?" Sara asked.

"I need to talk to Mother about something," Wendy answered. She went out into the hall. Sara and Susanna's mother was coming down the hall with their little brother Gilbert. "Are you girls having a nice time?" their mother asked with a smile.

Wendy looked up at Sister Amy with a troubled look. Mother was sitting in the living room at a place where she could see Wendy. She saw Wendy's troubled face. She stood up and came too, and Sister Esther followed.

The two mothers stepped into the room just as Sara was stuffing the book back into its place on the shelf.

"Sara, have you been snooping into Sister Esther's things?" her mother asked sternly.

Sara hung her head.

"We will need to talk about this when we get home," Sara's mother told her. "You know that Father and I want you to learn not to get into other people's things."

"I guess I should put those books in a place where they wouldn't be so tempting to little ones," Sister Esther apologized.

"No," Sister Amy answered. "The fault is with the children. They must learn to leave other people's things alone."

Sara was extra quiet and sober for the rest of the evening. Wendy felt sorry for her. "Probably Sara will be punished," she thought.

On the way home Mother asked, "Wendy, were you coming to tell me about the book that Sara got out of the cupboard?"

Wendy nodded. "I did not think it was a book that you would want me to look at," she said. "It was a book for big people, wasn't it?"

"Yes, it was," Mother answered. "I am very

glad that you were going to tell me about it. That is the right thing for children to do when they have a problem."

"I think Sara is probably going to be punished," Wendy said soberly.

"We will let Sara's parents take care of that," Father answered seriously. "When children get into things that aren't their business, or if they do things that they know their parents wouldn't be pleased with, then they need to be punished. If you learn to be honest and not hide things from Father and Mother when you are young, it will be easier for you to be honest when you are older too."

"That is how I want to be," Wendy said soberly. "I don't want to hide things from you and Mother."

"That is good," Father commended.

20.

Whose Business?

"Come, Sharon, I want to comb your hair," Mother said. "In half an hour we must leave for church."

Sharon laid down the book she had been looking at and came skipping to Mother. She sat down on the chair Mother had pulled out from the table.

"Sharon, did you know that today is Rachel's birthday?" Mother asked as she untwisted a rubber band from Sharon's hair. "Rachel's mother invited our family to their house for dinner."

"Oh, goody." Sharon clapped her hands. "Now Rachel is four like me, isn't she, Mother? May I give her a birthday card?"

"Yes, you are right; Rachel is four years old now," Mother answered. "And, yes, you may give her a card. There is a box of cards on my dresser. When I'm finished combing your hair, you may look at them and choose one that you like for Rachel."

As soon as Mother was finished combing her hair, Sharon jumped off the chair and headed for Mother's bedroom, where she found the box of cards. She took them to the living room and sat down on the couch to look at them.

"I like this one best," she decided, choosing one with two little kittens peeking out of a basket. She took an envelope from the bottom of the box and then put the rest of the cards back into the box.

"Mother, can you help me write Rachel's name on my card?" Sharon asked.

"Bring me a piece of scrap paper from your drawer, and I will write her name for you. Then you can copy it," Mother said as she tied little Andrew's shoe.

"This says, 'Dear Rachel,'" Mother explained,

writing the two words on her paper. "You can write this at the top. Then you can write 'From,' like this, at the bottom. And then write your name. You can do that all by yourself."

Sharon sat down at the table and carefully copied the words from Mother's paper. Last of all she carefully printed her name. "I'm all done!" she announced to Mother.

"Good," Mother said. "I'll put the card in my Bible. When we get to Rachel's house, you may give it to her. Now go and get your sweater. Father will soon be ready to go."

Sharon hurried to the closet where Mother kept the Sunday coats and sweaters. She found her sweater and slipped it on.

"I'm ready to go to the car," Mother said, picking up baby Philip from his infant seat. "Sharon, you may carry my Bible if you are very careful."

Sharon picked up Mother's Bible and carried it to the car. She knew that Rachel's birthday card and some other papers were inside the Bible, and she was careful not to let them fall out.

Soon Father came out to the car too, and the family was on their way to church.

When church was over, Sharon visited for a

while with her friend Darla. Before long Mother tapped her shoulder. "Father is ready to go," she said.

Soon they were heading for Rachel's house. Sharon held tightly to the card. She could hardly wait to give it to Rachel.

When they arrived at Rachel's house, Rachel was sitting on the porch swing. Janelle, another one of Sharon's friends, was sitting beside her. On Rachel's lap lay several envelopes, and she was opening one.

"Hi, Rachel," Sharon said. "Happy birthday." She laid the card on Rachel's lap.

"Thank you," Rachel said, smiling at Sharon. "Now I have six cards. Oh, look! This one is from Darla. Isn't it cute?" The card had a picture of a little girl holding a bouquet of flowers.

Father and Mother went into the house. Sharon reached out and picked up one of Rachel's cards. "May I open this one?" she asked.

Rachel was busy opening the next card and did not answer. Sharon began to tear the envelope open.

"Sharon, don't," Janelle said, trying to grab the card. "That's Rachel's, not yours."

"But Rachel has six cards. I can open just one," Sharon said, holding tightly to the card.

Rachel reached for the card. "Give it here, please, Sharon. It's mine."

Sharon's mother heard the fuss and came out onto the porch. "What's going on out here?"

"Sharon won't give Rachel her card," Janelle explained. "She started to open it, and I told her it's not hers."

"Janelle is right, Sharon," Mother said. "Give the card to Rachel."

Slowly Sharon handed the card to Rachel.

"Thank you," Rachel said sweetly.

On the way home that afternoon, Mother turned and looked at Sharon. "Sharon, why did you take Rachel's card?"

Sharon looked down at her lap. "Well, . . . Rachel had six cards, so I thought she could let me open just one. I wasn't going to keep it."

"If it was your birthday, don't you think you would like to open your own cards?" Mother asked kindly.

Sharon nodded her head slowly. "It's fun to have a birthday and open my cards," she said.

"And don't you think Rachel likes to open her own cards too?" Father asked. "Remember, the Bible says, 'And as ye would that men should do to you, do ye also to them likewise.'"

"The Bible also says, 'Do your own business,'" Mother added. "You must never open someone else's mail unless he gives you permission to do it. It was kind of Rachel to let you and Janelle enjoy her cards too, but opening the cards was Rachel's business, not yours. Do you understand?"

"Yes, Mother," Sharon answered. "I won't do it again. I want to be kind and do my own business."

"Never forget that," Father said, smiling kindly at Sharon. "We always want to obey God by doing what the Bible says."

21.

Micah's Conscience

Micah hopped off his tricycle as Father's pickup drove into the lane. He always looked forward to evenings when Father came home from work.

Micah ran toward the pickup when Father had stopped in front of the garage. Then he stared in surprise. He saw a little brown head with two floppy ears inside the window. Two big brown eyes were looking out at him.

"Father!" he squealed. "A puppy! Where did you get him? Is he ours?"

Father smiled as he lifted the squirming brown puppy out of the pickup. "Yes, she is ours," Father answered. "I got her for you. I stopped in at Brother Allen's on my way home from work. Their dog had pups several weeks ago, and Brother Allen asked if I wanted one. I looked at them and decided to get this one for you. You are getting big enough to take good care of a puppy."

Father handed the puppy to Micah. Micah's brown eyes sparkled as he hugged his new puppy. "Thank you, Father!" he exclaimed. "I am going to call her Sheba, like Mae's dog in *Kitten in the Well*. That would be a good name, wouldn't it?"

"Yes, that's a good name for your new pet," Father said with a smile. "Now I want to tell you something, Micah. Come with me." Father lifted a brown-and-white bag from the bed of the pickup and headed toward the barn.

Micah followed Father. Father stopped in the entryway in the barn and set the bag on the floor. "This is a bag of dog food for Sheba," Father explained. He tore the bag open and showed Micah what was in it. "Every morning and every evening you may give Sheba one scoop of this. But those are the only times that she needs dog food. Mother will give you bones and other table scraps to feed her sometimes."

"Okay," Micah answered. "It will be fun to take care of Sheba." He petted the brown puppy in his arms. Sheba sniffed at his shirt and gave a little bark.

Father laughed. "I think Sheba is saying, 'I like you.'"

For several weeks Micah faithfully fed Sheba every morning and evening. He remembered that Father had said that was all the food Sheba needed besides Mother's table scraps.

But one day Sheba and Micah were playing in the barn. It was almost dinnertime, and Micah was getting hungry. As he walked past the bag of dog food, Micah thought, "Sheba is probably hungry too." He looked at the bag a little longer.

"But Father said you should only feed her in the morning and in the evening," a little voice inside reminded him.

Micah stood there for a moment, undecided. Then he slowly opened the bag. He scooped out some food and put it into Sheba's dish. Sheba gobbled it up hungrily. Usually Micah liked to watch Sheba eat, but it was not much fun this time. He knew he had disobeyed.

"Micah, dinnertime!" he heard Mother call.

Micah put the scoop back into the bag and ran to the house.

All afternoon Micah did not feel happy. He sat on the swing under the shade tree for a long time. Sheba nudged him with her nose, begging him to play, but he did not feel like playing. He was glad when it was time to go to bed that night.

The next morning when Micah awoke, he remembered the dog food again. Tears filled his eyes, but he brushed them away quickly. He got dressed, combed his hair, and hurried downstairs for breakfast.

After breakfast the family gathered in the living room for devotions. "This morning we are going to read Daniel 1," Father said. "Karen, it is your turn to read first."

When all the verses had been read, Father said, "Daniel was a brave young man, doing right when the others were doing wrong. He trusted God, and God took care of him.

"There is something inside of us that tells us what is right and wrong," Father continued. "When it is trained according to God's Word, it makes us feel happy when we do right, and it makes us feel bad when we do wrong. Luke, what is that called?"

"Our conscience," ten-year-old Luke answered.

"Right," Father answered. "Daniel listened to his conscience. He had learned that God's Word said that he should not eat the king's meat, and he obeyed. Children," Father continued seriously, "any time that any of you has something that bothers you, we want you to come to Mother or me. Don't let it keep bothering you. If you don't take care of the things that trouble you, it will be harder for you to hear God calling you when you are older. It will be easier for you to disobey God."

Micah listened soberly to what Father said. A tear slipped down his cheek.

"What's wrong, Micah?" Father asked kindly.

"Yesterday I—I gave Sheba some dog food when it wasn't morning or evening," Micah said. "I thought she was hungry, but . . . but I'm sorry for disobeying you, Father."

Father looked kindly at Micah. "I am glad you told me, son. Your conscience was making you unhappy, wasn't it?"

Micah nodded.

"Since you told me yourself, I will not punish you this time," Father said. "But if it happens again, you will need to be punished. The next time you are tempted to do something like that, don't just stand there and think about it. Walk away and do something else that you know is right. Then you will not get into trouble. We want you to learn to make right choices like Daniel did in our story."

Micah nodded. He felt much better. He was glad he had told Father all about it. "The next time I will obey like Daniel did," he thought as the family knelt together for prayer.

22.

Lois and the Bribe

Lois wriggled excitedly as Father turned the car in Grandma's lane. "I like to go to Grandma Kline's house," she said.

Grandma Kline was not really Lois's grandmother, but she was a very dear old lady. Most of the children at church called her Grandma. Grandma Kline loved to have children come to her house, and Lois and her friends were always happy to go there.

"Come in, come in," Grandma welcomed from the doorway.

"That's what we're doing," Father chuckled. They all shook hands with Grandma as they filed past her into the house.

"Oh, are you here too?" Lois asked when she saw her friend Rosemary.

"Yes," Rosemary answered. "I was happy when Grandma told me that she had invited your family too."

Soon dinner was ready, and everyone sat down to enjoy Grandma's delicious chicken and noodle casserole and cherry pie.

When dinner was over, Rosemary suggested, "Let's play house in the basement."

"Yes, let's," Lois agreed eagerly. She loved to play in Grandma's basement. Grandma had one little corner fixed up like a house for little girls to play in when they came.

The two girls scampered down the stairs.

"I'll take this doll with the broken nose," Lois said. "Do you want this other one, Rosemary?"

"Okay," Rosemary answered, picking up the dark-haired doll. "My baby is sleepy. I must rock her." She sat down in the little rocking chair.

"It's time to make dinner," Lois decided. She opened the little cupboard and took out two

kettles. "What shall we have?"

"Oh, here comes Martha," Rosemary said. "Martha, are you going to play with us?" Martha was eleven years old, and she did not often play with the little girls.

"Oh, maybe for a while," said Martha. "What can I do?"

"Do you want to be the mother?" Lois asked. "We can be your little girls."

"Okay," Martha agreed. "And the doll that Rosemary is holding will be our baby. Her name is Kristen."

After a while Martha got tired of playing house. She walked over to the shelves where Grandma kept her canned things. "I'm going to climb up on these shelves," she said.

Lois's eyes got big. "You can't do that!" she exclaimed.

"Oh, yes, I can," Martha said. "See?" She took hold of the third shelf with both hands and put her feet on the bottom shelf. Then she lifted her foot to put it on the next shelf. Suddenly, *crash!* Her foot bumped some jars on the bottom shelf, and two of them fell from the shelf and landed on the floor. They broke into many pieces, and tomato juice spread in a big puddle on the floor.

"Oh, Martha!" Rosemary gasped. "See what you did!"

Martha climbed down and looked at the mess she had made. She looked very sober.

"What will Grandma say?" Lois added.

Martha lifted her chin. "Grandma won't have to know I did it," she said. "You girls won't tell, will you?"

Lois and Rosemary looked at each other uncertainly.

"Listen," Martha said, "I have two little candy bars in my purse. If you promise not to tell Grandma that I broke the jars, I will give you each a candy bar." She looked from Lois to Rosemary and then back to Lois again.

"Okay," Lois said slowly. "I won't tell."

"I won't either," Rosemary promised.

"Let's go outside," Martha suggested. "My purse is in our car. I will get the candy for you, and then I'll push you on the swings."

Lois and Rosemary followed Martha outside. Martha got the candy bars from her purse. She handed one to Lois and one to Rosemary.

Lois opened her wrapper and took a tiny bite. M-m-m! The soft sweetness melted in her mouth.

When the candy had disappeared, Lois and Rosemary followed Martha to the swings. They both sat down, and Martha pushed them high. Usually Lois enjoyed being pushed on the swings. But this time she was not feeling happy. She was feeling very troubled.

Soon Martha saw her family going to the car. Martha ran to join them. "Good-bye, girls!" she called to Lois and Rosemary.

"Good-bye!" Rosemary and Lois called back.

A little later Rosemary's mother called, "Lois, Rosemary, come here please."

"I wonder what she wants," Rosemary said. "Do you think they saw the broken jars?"

"I don't know," Lois said miserably. "I wish I had never promised not to tell."

"I know," Rosemary agreed. "But what shall we do? We already ate the candy."

Rosemary's mother led the girls down to the basement. Lois's mother and Grandma were standing by the broken jars.

"Girls, did you break these jars when you were playing down here?" Lois's mother asked.

The girls shook their heads.

"Do you know what happened?" she asked, turning to Lois.

Lois looked down at the floor. Her lower lip trembled, but she did not answer.

"Come with me, Lois," Mother instructed. She led Lois to a little room in the corner of the basement.

"Now tell me what happened," she kindly encouraged her.

Slowly the whole story came out. "Martha gave us candy and told us not to tell," she finished unhappily. "But we wished we wouldn't have promised. It made us feel bad."

"I am glad you understand that you did wrong," Mother said. "The candy Martha offered you is called a bribe. She knew that she should tell Grandma about the broken jars, but she didn't want to. And she didn't want you or Rosemary to tell either. You should have told Martha that you would not make such a promise. We must always do right, and we should never take a gift from someone who wants us to promise to do wrong."

"I'm sorry, Mother," Lois said. "Should I tell Grandma about it even if I promised that I wouldn't?"

"Yes, you should," Mother answered. "God wants us to keep our promises, but this time you made a promise that was not good. That is wrong. The next time you must remember not to make such a promise."

"I will try," Lois promised. She felt much better already.

"I will need to talk to Martha's mother about this too," Mother added. Then she and Lois went back to join the others.

Rosemary's mother had talked to Rosemary too. Two sober girls told Grandma the whole story.

"You girls learned an important lesson today," Grandma said, smiling lovingly at Lois and Rosemary. "It is important to always do what is right even when others want us to do something wrong. And you also learned that it is never right to accept a gift for doing wrong, didn't you?"

Both girls nodded their heads as they returned Grandma's smile. "Mother said that is called a bribe," Lois said.

"That's right," Grandma agreed.

"Now you may go and play again," Rosemary's mother said.

"I feel so much better since we told our mothers and Grandma about it," Lois said to Rosemary as they headed back to the swings. "That candy tasted good, but it would have been much better to do what was right and not had the candy. I don't want to ever take anyone's bribe again."

"I don't either," Rosemary agreed. "Mother said that God can help us to do right even if others want us to do wrong."

Two happy girls smiled at each other as

they sat down on the swings. Now they could enjoy their play because everything had been made right.

23.

Why Did She Cry?

"'I was glad, I was glad when they said unto me, / Let us go to the house of the Lord,'" Verna sang joyfully as she rode in the back seat of the station wagon.

"'We shall stand, we shall stand, stand within Thy gates . . .'" Father and Mother joined in when she started the second verse.

"Mother, I like that song because it is a going-to-church song," Verna said. "I like to go to church. Sunday is my best day."

"I am glad that you like Sunday," Father said.

"God planned that we should work on the other six days of the week. We are happy on those days too because we are serving God. But Sunday is a special day for us to rest and worship God. Mother and I like Sunday too."

Soon they arrived at church. Verna got out and followed Mother to the church house. She slipped out of her coat and handed it to Mother. Mother hung it on a hanger. Then Mother turned around and greeted several sisters with a holy kiss.

"Good morning, Verna," Sister Janice said, reaching out to shake her hand. Verna smiled shyly and shook hands with Sister Janice. She liked Sister Janice. Sister Janice was always friendly, and after church she often talked to Verna and her friends.

"Come, Verna. It's time to go in and sit down," Mother said.

Sister Janice went first, and Mother and Verna followed her. Verna sat next to Sister Janice, and Mother sat on the other side of Verna.

Soon the song leader walked to the front of the church. "Number 179," he announced. The congregation began to sing, "'Welcome, sweet day of rest, / That saw the Lord arise . . .'"

Verna helped with the parts of the song that she knew. "That song must be about Sunday," she thought. "Father said that Sunday is a day of rest."

When Brother Mark got up to preach, Verna sat quietly and listened. Sometimes Brother Mark told Bible stories that she could understand.

After a while, Verna looked up at Sister Janice. Sister Janice smiled at her, but then Verna saw something that surprised her. Sister Janice had tears in her eyes!

"I wonder why she is crying," Verna thought. She looked at Mother, but Mother was listening to Brother Mark. "I will ask her when we get home," Verna decided. "I know that is the way Mother wants me to do."

After church Sister Janice talked for a while with Mother. Verna smiled at her friend Naomi, who had been sitting behind her and Mother. Naomi began telling her about the new twin goats on their farm. It did not seem long at all until Mother said, "Come, Verna. Father is ready to go."

When they were on their way home, Verna remembered her question. "Mother, I looked at Sister Janice one time during church. She

smiled at me, but she had tears in her eyes. What was wrong?"

Mother turned slightly in her seat so that she could see Verna. "Janice was talking to me about it after church," she explained. "Verna, do you remember the first time Janice came to our church?"

Verna wrinkled her forehead. "That was a long time ago, wasn't it, Mother? She wore pants then, didn't she?"

"Yes, she did," Mother replied. "Sister Janice's parents are not Christians. When she was growing up, she watched television. We know that there are many things on television that do not please God. She also saw her parents and others do many things that do not please God, and she learned to do those things too. She was not a Christian, so she did not have God's power to think about right things either." Mother paused.

"When Sister Janice gave her heart to the Lord, Jesus made her heart clean, and now He helps her to do right things and to think right thoughts. But sometimes Satan tries to make her remember the things she used to do and think about. God helps her to do what is right, but it is not always easy."

Verna sat quietly as Mother talked. "I am glad you and Father are Christians," she said. "I am glad you do not teach me to do bad things."

"Yes, we need to thank God for Christian homes," Mother said. "Satan wants all of us to do wrong things, but God helps those who want to do right."

"Mother, we can pray for Sister Janice, can't we?" Verna asked.

"Yes, we certainly can," Mother agreed. "She asked me this morning if I would pray for her, and I said I will."

That evening at bedtime Mother and Verna knelt beside Verna's bed to pray. "Dear God," Verna prayed, "thank You for Your plan for Sunday. Thank You that we can go to church. Thank You for Father and Mother and my Sunday school teacher, Sister Ruth. And thank You, God, that Sister Janice learned to love You. Help her to forget the bad things she learned about, and help her to think about good things that please You. In Jesus' Name. Amen."

Mother prayed too. She prayed for Sister Janice and asked God to be with her and make her strong. Then they got up from their knees.

"I am glad that we prayed for Sister Janice, Mother," Verna said as Mother tucked her into bed. "God will help her, won't He?"

"Yes, she truly wants to obey God, so we know that He will help her," Mother answered. "God has promised to help those who want to do right. Good night, Verna."

"Good night," Verna answered as she snuggled under her covers. Soon she was fast asleep.

24.

No Salve for Samuel

"Carolyn, please go to the bedroom and get a clean suit for Samuel," Mother said as she lifted three-week-old Samuel from his bassinet and carried him to the table.

Carolyn hurried to the bedroom and soon returned with a little blue suit. She watched as Mother slipped Samuel's sleeper off and put his suit on. "Oh, look, Mother!" she exclaimed. "Samuel has a big red spot on his neck!"

"Yes, I saw that he has," Mother answered. "I put some salve on it last evening and again this morning, but it doesn't seem to be helping. If it isn't better by tomorrow, I'll have to call Dr. Jergens." Mother picked up the tube of salve. Samuel whimpered as Mother gently rubbed salve on the sore.

"Poor baby," Carolyn said. "That looks like it would hurt."

"I know," Mother agreed.

That evening when the family was gathered for devotions, Father asked, "What shall we pray for this evening?"

"That God would heal Samuel's sore if it is His will," Carolyn suggested. She looked at sweet little Samuel sleeping in Mother's arms.

"Yes," Father agreed.

Mother and several of the other children gave their prayer requests. When the family knelt for prayer, everyone remembered to pray for Samuel.

The next afternoon when Carolyn and her brothers came home from school, they sat down at the table for their snack.

"Is Samuel's sore any better, Mother?" Eldon asked as he picked up a cookie from the plate that Mother had placed on the table for them.

"No, it isn't," Mother answered. "When he woke up this morning, I checked it. It looked worse than it did yesterday, and it was bleeding a little. I called Dr. Jergens. Father plans to pick up some salve at the drugstore this evening on his way home from work."

"Mother, did you see how much it is snowing?" Carolyn asked excitedly. "Sister Edna drove the school van today. She almost went in the ditch when we came down that big hill close to Earl Clark's place!"

"Yes, there was a big patch of ice near the bottom of the hill, and she slid around," Eldon added. "I thought she was going to go in the ditch, but she made it down the hill."

"Oh," Mother said, "that was scary, wasn't it? I'm thankful that the Lord protected you."

"Father's home!" Carolyn called joyfully an hour later. "I hope he remembered Samuel's medicine."

"It's not medicine, Carolyn," Eldon corrected her. "It's salve to put on his sore spot."

"Well, whatever." Carolyn shrugged her shoulders and hurried to open the door for Father.

Father drove the car into the garage and stepped out.

"Did you get the . . . salve for Samuel?" Carolyn asked.

"Yes, here it is." Father held up a tiny glass jar for Carolyn to see.

Just then Father's foot slipped on a wet spot on the floor. As he tried to regain his balance, the jar flew out of his hand and crashed against the wall of the garage. Carolyn watched in horror as it broke into tiny pieces.

"Oh, no! Now see what I did," Father said. "We won't be able to use that salve. Carolyn, please bring me the broom and dustpan, and I'll clean up this glass."

Carolyn hurried to the kitchen closet and grabbed the broom and dustpan.

"What happened?" Mother asked as Carolyn headed for the garage again.

"Father almost fell out in the garage," Carolyn explained quickly. "The jar with Samuel's salve in it crashed against the wall and broke."

Carolyn went out to the garage. Father had gotten a rag from the corner of the garage to wipe up the salve. Before long the mess was cleaned up.

After supper Father put on his coat and headed toward the door.

"Where are you going, Father?" Carolyn asked.

"I'm going to the drugstore to get more salve for Samuel," Father answered. "Mother called the doctor, and he said he will call the drug-store with another prescription."

"May I go along?" Carolyn pleaded.

"I don't think so," Father replied. "The way it is snowing, I think I'd better go alone."

It seemed like a long time before Carolyn saw Father's headlights coming in the driveway.

"Did you get some more salve?" she asked eagerly as Father stepped inside the kitchen. "Where is it?" she asked, seeing Father's empty hands.

"I wasn't able to get any," Father said. "The electricity is out at that end of town. When I got there, they were guiding people out of the store with flashlights. I waited for fifteen or twenty minutes, but the electricity didn't go back on. So I came home without any salve."

"What are we going to do now?" Carolyn asked. "Samuel needs that salve real badly. His sore looks awful this evening."

"The Lord must have a purpose for allowing things to happen like this," Mother said. "Maybe He wants us to depend completely on Him rather than on the salve to heal Samuel."

"That's right," Father agreed. "We will pray again tonight and ask the Lord to heal the sore if it is His will."

When they knelt for prayer during family worship, each of the children and their parents remembered baby Samuel's need in prayer. Then they went to bed, trusting the Lord to do what was best.

"Mother, is Samuel's sore any better?" Carolyn asked anxiously as she entered the kitchen the next morning.

"Yes, I think it is," Mother answered. "It doesn't look as raw as it did yesterday. The Lord is answering our prayer."

At the breakfast table, Father prayed, ". . . And thank You, Lord, that Samuel's sore is getting better. Help us to always remember that You are the one who heals our bodies. In Jesus' Name. Amen."

"Father, didn't God want Mother to use the salve?" Carolyn asked as Father slid an egg from the platter onto her plate.

"Well," Father began, "God gave us doctors and medicines, and many times He uses them to help us get better when we are sick. But sometimes it is easy for us to depend on them too much, and maybe we don't remember as we should that it is really God who heals. We don't really know why God kept us from being able to use the salve, but we do know that 'all things work together for good to them that love God.' We want to learn the lessons that God has for us. And I believe that one of these lessons is to trust God completely to heal Samuel, if that is His will."

The next two days Samuel's sore continued to get better. On the third day, Father got another jar of salve, and Mother used it several times. But the family knew that it was God, not the salve, who had healed Samuel's sore.

"I'm so glad Samuel's sore is healed," Carolyn said to Mother on Sunday morning.

"I am glad too," Mother agreed. "We need God so much for everything. I am thankful that we have a God who loves us very much and answers our prayers."

Carolyn nodded as she bent down and gave her little brother a kiss on his cheek.

25.

What Will Tabitha Do?

Henry stretched and yawned. "This book is so interesting," he thought as he turned another page of *Storytime With Grandma.*

"Come here, please, Henry," Mother called from the kitchen.

Slowly he obeyed. He laid down his book and walked to the kitchen.

"Please take these scraps out to the pigpen," Mother instructed, handing Henry a bowl of scraps.

Henry sighed as he took the bowl from

Mother. He did not feel like taking out the scraps. He looked at his younger sister Tabitha, who was sitting at the table coloring. "What is Tabitha going to do?" he asked.

"When I'm done mixing up this cake, I am going to wash my baking dishes, and I want her to dry them for me," Mother answered.

Henry walked out to the pigpen. He climbed up onto the bottom rail and dumped the scraps over the fence. He laughed to himself as the three fat pigs came grunting over to his little pile of scraps. He liked to watch the funny pigs shove and push to get as much as possible.

When the pigs had gulped down all the scraps, Henry headed back to the house. "Here's your bowl, Mother," he said.

"Thank you, Henry," Mother said with a smile. "Now will you please run out and tell Father that Mr. Evans called? He wants to come over this evening to look at the baler that Father has for sale. If it doesn't suit Father, we are supposed to call him back."

Henry looked at Tabitha. She was still busy coloring.

"It's not fair that I have to work and she doesn't," he grumbled.

"Henry," Mother said firmly, "you are older than Tabitha, and it is right that you should be working sometimes when she isn't. I want you to go and do the job that I gave you. Tabitha will soon have a job to do too."

That evening Henry was playing on the floor with his blocks when Mother said, "It is almost bedtime, children. You have ten more minutes; then I want you to pick up your toys and start getting ready for bed."

Father looked up from the book he was reading. "I saw a ball and a toy truck out in the yard when I came in," he said. "Henry, run out and bring them in, please. Go right away so you don't forget."

Henry looked at Tabitha. "What's Tabitha going to do?"

Father frowned. "Henry, go at once and bring those toys into the house. Then I want to talk to you."

Henry hurried outside. He knew he had not obeyed cheerfully and promptly. Was Father going to punish him? He picked up the ball and the truck and went back into the house. He dropped the ball into the toy box and set the truck beside it. Then he walked slowly over to Father.

Father moved over to make room for Henry to sit on the arm of the chair beside him. Then he said, "Henry, Mother has been telling me that often when she asks you to do something for her, you ask what Tabitha will do."

Henry hung his head.

211

"In the Bible there is a story about a man named Peter," Father continued. "One day Peter and his friends went fishing. When they returned to the shore, Jesus had a meal ready for them. After they ate, Jesus talked to Peter. He said, 'Follow me.' Peter turned around and saw John, another disciple. Peter said, 'Lord, and what shall this man do?'

"Jesus didn't answer Peter's question. He said, 'If I will that he tarry till I come, what is that to thee? follow thou me.' That might be a little hard for you to understand, but what Jesus meant was that Peter should not have asked what John was going to do. It was none of Peter's business. Jesus wanted Peter to follow Him without asking what John would do.

"When Mother or I give you a job to do," Father said, "I want you to remember that. It is for Mother and me to decide what Tabitha will do. Your job is to obey and to cheerfully do your own work. If this habit does not stop, you will need to be punished. Do you understand?"

Henry slowly nodded his head.

"Okay, now go and wash your face and brush your teeth," Father instructed. "I think Mother is ready for story time."

The next morning after breakfast, Mother

started to wash the dishes. "Henry, I want you to dry the dishes for me," she said.

Henry looked at Tabitha. She was sitting in her little rocking chair, rocking her doll. "What is—" he began. Then suddenly he remembered. He must cheerfully obey without asking what Tabitha was going to do. He walked over to the counter and picked up the tea towel.

Father was sitting at the table, writing a letter. "Henry, I am glad to see that you are trying to overcome your bad habit," Father said. "You are much happier when you do your own business, aren't you?"

Henry nodded. He felt happy because he had done right. From now on he would try to mind his own business and not worry about Tabitha's jobs.

26.

A Home for Amy and Anthony

Jessica rocked her doll baby gently in her arms. "I like our little house under the weeping willow tree," she said, looking at the branches that hung almost to the ground around their cozy house.

"I do too," Sue Ann agreed.

Jessica laid her baby in its bed of pine needles. "I'm going to ask Mother if we may have some crackers for our dinner," she said.

"Okay," Sue Ann answered, looking up from feeding her baby.

Jessica skipped toward the house. She opened the screen door and began, "Mother, may we—" She stopped suddenly. Mother was talking on the telephone, and Jessica saw that she had tears in her eyes.

"Oh, I'm sorry to hear that," Mother was saying. "Yes, we will be glad to come for supper this evening."

Jessica waited for a few moments, but Mother was not done talking yet. "I'd better go out to Sue Ann," she decided to herself.

"Did you get crackers?" Sue Ann asked as Jessica stooped down and entered their little house.

"No," Jessica said slowly. "Mother is talking on the telephone. I think something sad happened because she is crying. But I think we're going to someone's house for supper too."

Sue Ann looked as puzzled as Jessica felt.

"Jessica! Sue Ann!" the girls heard Mother calling a few minutes later. "Come here, please!"

Jessica laid down the doll dress that she had been folding, and Sue Ann put her doll in its little bed. Then they headed for the house.

Mother was sitting at the kitchen table when

they entered the kitchen. "Girls, we are invited to the Eberly's for supper this evening," Mother told the girls.

"Oh, good!" Both girls were happy about that. The Eberlys had two little foster children.

Amy was two years old, and Anthony was one. Jessica and Sue Ann loved to play with them.

"But, Mother, why are you sad?" Jessica asked.

"Girls, do you remember when Amy and Anthony came to live with the Eberlys?" Mother asked.

Jessica and Sue Ann nodded.

"You said that their mother couldn't take care of them then, so Brother Glen and Sister Martha were going to take care of them for a while," Jessica said.

"That's right," Mother answered. "And their mother still isn't able to care for them. But one of their aunts wants to have them. Their aunt isn't a Christian. Sister Martha said that she smokes cigarettes and uses bad words when she talks."

"Oh." Jessica's eyes grew big. "Can't Brother Glen and Sister Martha just say no, and that they want to keep Amy and Anthony?"

"No, they can't," Mother answered. "The other lady is their aunt, so if she wants to care for them, she will be allowed to have them."

Jessica's eyes filled with tears. "But I don't want Amy and Anthony to go to that lady's house. They won't learn about God there, will they?"

"I am sure they will not be taught to love God and obey the Bible," Mother answered sadly.

"Amy likes to sing 'Jesus Loves Me,'" Sue Ann said. "Maybe the lady won't like that."

"I don't know if she will or not," Mother answered. "Shall we kneel down and ask God to take care of Amy and Anthony?"

The girls nodded.

"Can we ask God not to let that lady take them?" Jessica asked.

"Yes," Mother answered, "but we must remember to pray 'if it is Your will.'"

Jessica and Sue Ann followed Mother to the living room. Together the three knelt in front of the sofa.

Jessica prayed first. "Dear God, thank You for Amy and Anthony. They are so sweet. We want them to grow up to love You. Please let them stay at Brother Glen and Sister Martha's house if it is Your will."

Then Sue Ann prayed, "Dear God, please take care of Amy and Anthony. Help them to stay at Brother Glen's house if it is Your will. In Jesus' Name. Amen."

Then Mother prayed. She also asked God to watch over Amy and Anthony. She prayed that God would help them to grow up to love and obey Him.

"Wouldn't God want Amy and Anthony to stay at Brother Glen's house?" Jessica asked as they rose from their knees. "He wouldn't want them to learn bad things at the other lady's house, would He?"

"God wants all children to grow up to love and serve Him," Mother explained. "But you girls remember the story of Adam and Eve in the Bible, don't you?"

Both girls nodded. Jessica wondered why Mother asked them that.

"When Adam and Eve disobeyed God in the Garden of Eden, many sinful things began to happen in the world," Mother explained. "A while after Adam and Eve sinned, Cain killed Abel. Even later, some proud men built a tower called Babel. They wanted the tower to reach up to heaven. They wanted people to praise them. Many people began to worship idols."

Jessica nodded, and Mother continued her story. "Because we all live together here on the earth, many times people who are obeying God have to suffer when others disobey. Abel was a godly man, but he died because Cain disobeyed

God and killed Abel. Many children do not have the chance to grow up in happy Christian homes because their parents do not love God. God is sad to see this happen, just as we are sad. But God does not make anyone be a Christian."

"But people who aren't Christians can't go to heaven, can they?" Sue Ann asked.

"No, they can't," Mother answered. "Someday God will punish those who do not obey Him. All Christians and all little children will live in heaven with God forever."

"We will be happy in heaven." Jessica's eyes sparkled.

"We can pray for Amy and Anthony even if they go to live with their aunt," Mother added. "Even if we can't be with them, God will be with them. Now, I need two girls to help me fold the laundry so that we can go away for supper this evening."

"We will!" both girls responded willingly.

Later that evening, Jessica and Sue Ann and their parents sadly said good-bye to Anthony and Amy. Jessica watched Mother give them both a hug. She saw that Mother had tears in her eyes, and so did Sister Martha. Jessica felt tears coming to her eyes as she gave Amy a good-bye kiss.

Everyone was quiet as they drove home. "It seems so sad that we might not see Amy and Anthony again," Jessica said.

"Yes, it does," Mother agreed. "But we hope that when they grow up, they will want to love and serve God."

When they arrived home, Jessica and Sue Ann went to their bedroom to get ready for bed. Mother came to pray with them, and then she tucked them in. "Good night, girls," she said.

"Good night," they replied together.

Jessica lay awake in the dark for a long time. She could tell by Sue Ann's breathing that she had fallen asleep. But Jessica could not sleep. She was thinking about Amy and Anthony. Tomorrow they would have to leave Brother Glen's house and go to a strange home—a home where the lady smoked and used bad words. "I would be scared," Jessica thought. "I wonder if the lady will be nice to them."

Jessica felt the tears coming to her eyes again. She began to sob. She buried her face in her pillow so that she would not waken her sister.

Jessica lifted her head when she heard the door open.

"Aren't you asleep yet, Jessica?" Mother whispered.

Jessica shook her head.

"What's wrong?" Mother asked kindly.

"I—I keep thinking about Amy and Anthony," Jessica answered between sobs. "I don't want them to go to their aunt's house. I want them to stay with Brother Glen and Sister Martha."

"So do I," Mother said softly. "I feel sad for them too." In the light that came in from the hallway, Jessica could see the tears in Mother's eyes.

"We prayed for Amy and Anthony," Mother reminded Jessica. "We must trust Jesus to take care of them. He loves them very much. He feels very sad too about children who do not have happy Christian homes. We must keep on praying for them."

Jessica smiled through her tears. It made her feel better to think that Jesus understood how sad she felt. "May I pray for Amy and Anthony here in my bed?" she asked.

"Surely you may," Mother answered. "God is pleased whenever we talk to Him. Do you think you can go to sleep now, dear?"

"I think so," Jessica answered.

When Mother left the room, Jessica prayed a quiet little prayer to God for Amy and Anthony. She did not feel so worried anymore. Soon she fell asleep.

The next day Jessica and Sue Ann were helping Mother bake cookies when the telephone rang. Mother answered it. Jessica watched Mother's face. She looked very happy.

"Praise the Lord!" Mother exclaimed. "This is an answer to prayer."

"Something good must have happened," Sue Ann whispered to Jessica.

Jessica nodded. "I wonder what it is."

When Mother hung up the telephone, she gathered her two girls into her arms. "Oh, girls, that was Sister Martha. She said that Amy and Anthony will not be leaving after all. The aunt has decided that taking care of two children would be too much for her."

Jessica clapped her hands. "Oh, I'm so glad, glad, glad!" she sang.

"God doesn't always answer our prayers in this way," Mother said. "Maybe another time Anthony and Amy will have to leave. But this time God worked it out for them to be able to stay. Brother Glen and Sister Martha will have more time to teach them about God and the

Bible. Come, girls, let's thank God for answering our prayers."

As they rose from their knees a few minutes later, Jessica's heart felt all bubbly and happy. "I feel so happy, I could just sing and sing and sing!" she exclaimed.

"Then let's sing," Mother said with a smile. "Shall we sing 'Whisper a Prayer in the Morning'?"

"Yes, let's," the girls agreed.

Three joyful voices joined together in singing the first verse. Then they began the second verse: "'God answers prayer in the morning, / God answers prayer at noon; / God answers prayer in the evening, / So keep your heart in tune.'"

When they had finished, Jessica said, "God really did answer our prayer just like the song says, didn't He, Mother?"

"He surely did," Mother answered. Jessica saw the glad light in Mother's eyes.

Several weeks later, Mother had more good news for the girls. "Brother Glen and Sister Martha are planning to adopt Amy and Anthony," she told them. "Their mother is very sick and will probably never be able to care for them."

"What does *adopt* mean?" Sue Ann wondered.

"When parents adopt a child, they take him for their very own," Mother explained. "Amy and Anthony's last name will be Eberly instead of Cruz."

"You mean then nobody can take them away again, like that lady was going to?" Jessica asked.

"They will be Brother Glen and Sister Martha's children, just like you and Sue Ann are our children," Mother answered. "Unless some accident or something happens, they will live with Brother Glen and Sister Martha until they are grown up."

"Sister Martha must be very happy," Jessica said thoughtfully.

"Yes, she is," Mother said.

"And we are too!" Sue Ann added.

"This is a very happy answer to our prayers, isn't it, Mother?" Jessica asked.

"It surely is," Mother answered, giving Jessica a tight squeeze. "We are so glad that Amy and Anthony can have a Christian home. It will soon be time for supper, and then we'll have family worship. We want to thank God for His answer to our prayers."

Two happy girls followed Mother to the kitchen to help her with supper.

27.

The Wrong Way to Give

"Now what shall I do next?" Angela asked herself as she closed the book she had been looking at. As she sat quietly, she could hear Mother in the kitchen singing. "'Oh, how I love Jesus! / Oh, how I love Jesus! / Oh, how I love Jesus! / Because He first loved me!'"

"I know what! I want to give Mother a special surprise. Maybe I could make a little card for her."

Angela looked down at the end table beside the couch. "What's this?" She picked up a folded piece of paper that was lying on the end table and opened it.

"Oh, it's the puppy that Clinton drew last night," Angela thought. "It is a pretty puppy. Mother would like a picture of a puppy, I am sure." Angela picked up the picture and walked out to the kitchen.

"Mother, guess what I have." Angela held her hands behind her back.

"I don't know," Mother answered. "Is it a pencil?"

Angela shook her head.

"Is it a book?"

"No, it's a picture, and it's for you!" Angela held out the folded piece of paper to Mother.

Angela watched eagerly as Mother looked at the picture. "This is a pretty puppy," Mother said. Then a frown crossed her face. "But isn't this the puppy that Clinton drew for Grandmother?"

Angela nodded. "But I knew you would like it. Clinton can draw another one."

"This picture isn't yours to give away, Angela," Mother said. "If you want to give me a gift, you must give me something that belongs to you. Put Clinton's picture back where you found it. Then you can draw a puppy for me."

Angela's lower lip quivered. "But I can't draw as nice as Clinton can."

"That's all right," Mother said kindly. "I will like your puppy anyway. Just do your best."

Slowly Angela walked to the living room. She put Clinton's picture away; then she took a piece of paper from the desk drawer. She sat down to draw a puppy for Mother.

When she was finished, she went to the kitchen again. "Here is a puppy for you, Mother," she said.

"Thank you, Angela," Mother said. "You did a very nice job."

Several days later Sister Anita came for a visit. Her five-year-old daughter, Louise, was with her.

"Would you like to play with the dolls?" Angela asked Louise.

"Yes, let's," Louise answered.

Soon the two girls were playing happily. As Angela sat rocking her baby, she thought, "I would like to give Louise a present. What could I give her?"

Angela looked around. Then she saw her sister Ruth's doll sitting on a chair. Ruth's doll was wearing the blue barrettes that Ruth had worn when she was a little girl.

"I could give those barrettes to Louise," Angela thought. "She would like them for her doll."

Angela put her doll on the rocking chair. She walked over to Ruth's doll. Carefully she took the blue barrettes from the doll's hair.

"Here, Louise, you may have these barrettes," Angela said.

"You mean to keep?" Louise took the blue barrettes that Angela was holding out to her.

"Yes," Angela answered.

"Thank you," Louise said. "They are pretty."

When Ruth came home from school that evening, Mother had a few jobs for her. Then Ruth said to Angela, "Shall we play with our dolls?"

"Yes!" Angela said, running to get her doll.

Ruth picked up her doll. "Why, what happened to her barrettes?" she exclaimed.

Mother walked into the living room. "Did you lose your doll's barrettes?" she asked.

Ruth nodded. "I am sure she had them on when I played with her the last time."

"Angela, you and Louise were playing dolls together today. Do you know what happened to the barrettes that Ruth had in her doll's hair?" Mother asked.

Angela looked down at the floor. "I—I gave them to Louise."

"You gave them to Louise!" Ruth exclaimed. "But they were mine!"

"Angela," Mother began kindly, "do you remember what I told you when you wanted to give me Clinton's puppy picture?"

Angela's eyes filled with tears. "That I shouldn't give someone else's things away."

"In the Bible there is a story about a poor man who had one little lamb," Mother began. "This lamb was very special to the man and his family. It ate the same food as the man's family did. The man and his family liked their little lamb very much.

"Nearby there lived a rich man who had many, many sheep. One day a visitor came to the rich man's house. The rich man wanted meat for his visitor. But instead of killing one of his own sheep, he took the poor man's sheep and cooked it for his visitor."

"That was mean!" Ruth exclaimed.

"Yes, that was very unkind," Mother agreed. "Even if the other man had not been poor, it would still not have been right for the rich man to take the lamb. God is pleased when we give gifts to others. But if we give to someone something that does not belong to us, that is stealing."

"I didn't know it was stealing," Angela said slowly. "I'm sorry, Mother . . . and Ruth."

"I want you to take your doll's barrettes and give them to Ruth," Mother instructed. "When we take something that belongs to someone else, God wants us to make it right."

Angela slowly took the brown barrettes from her doll's hair and handed them to Ruth.

"Also, after this I want you girls to ask me before you give a gift to someone else," Mother added.

"I will," Ruth promised.

"I will too," Angela agreed as she soberly stroked her doll's hair where the barrettes had been.

28.

The Biggest Number

"'Our day of school is over, / And we are going home; / Good-bye, good-bye, / Be always kind and true; / Good-bye, good-bye, / We will be kind and true,'" the students in Sister Marie's room sang joyfully.

"Row one is dismissed," Sister Marie said when the song was finished.

First grader Jeremy followed the others in his row out to the cloakroom. He quickly slipped into his jacket, grabbed his lunch box, and ran out to the waiting van. He sat down in his place beside little Galen's car seat.

"Hi, Galen," he said, touching Galen's soft cheek. Galen looked up at his big brother and cooed happily.

"Did you have a good day, Jeremy?" Mother asked as Jeremy fastened his seat belt.

"Oh, yes!" Jeremy answered. "Yesterday we had to write the numbers from one all the way to fifty. Now today we had to write the rest of the numbers up to one hundred. I think math is my favorite subject in school—besides recess." He grinned at Mother.

Jeremy's friend Luke climbed into the van and sat beside Jeremy. Soon all the children were in the van, and Mother pulled out the driveway.

"Do you know what the biggest number in all the world is?" Luke asked Jeremy.

"No, I don't," Jeremy answered. "Is it a trillion?"

"No, it's a googol," Luke answered.

"That's not true!" Jeremy disagreed. "There's no such number as a googol! You just made that up."

"No, I didn't," Luke said. "My brother Andrew told me."

"Well, that sure sounds like a made-up

word," Jeremy's sister Alice said. "I never heard of such a number."

"Well, there is," Luke insisted. "Andrew said so, and he knows lots and lots of things about numbers."

"What's going on, children?" Mother asked, looking in the rearview mirror.

"Luke says that the biggest number in all the world is a googol," Jeremy said. "It's not, is it, Mother?"

"Well, here we are at Luke's house now," Mother said. "We'll talk about this later, Jeremy. Let's not argue."

Luke and his sisters climbed out of the van and ran toward their house. Jeremy watched Luke running ahead of his sisters. He still was sure that there was no such number as a googol. Why, that was such a funny word!

When all the children except Jeremy and Alice had gotten out of the van, Jeremy moved to the front seat beside Mother. "Mother, is there really such a number as a googol?" he asked.

"I've never heard of such a number," Mother admitted. "But let's look it up in the dictionary when we get home."

When they arrived home, Jeremy and Alice

ran to the house. They plunked their lunch boxes on the table. Alice hurried to the living room and got the dictionary from the bookshelf. Jeremy watched as she turned the pages till she got to the letter *G*.

"Did you find it?" Mother asked, coming in the door with Galen in her arms.

"Not yet," Alice answered. "How is it spelled?"

"I'm not sure," Mother said. "Let's start with *g-o-o* and see what we can find." She moved her finger down the page. "Oh, here it is! *Googol*. It means the number one followed by one hundred zeroes."

"O-o-oh!" Alice exclaimed. "That would be a huge number, wouldn't it, Mother? It would take several lines on a paper to write it. How many zeroes does a trillion have?"

"It has twelve zeroes," Mother answered. "So a googol is a much, much larger number than a trillion."

"Does that mean that a googol is really the biggest number in the world?" Jeremy asked quietly.

"I don't think we can say that for sure," Mother answered. "I don't know what the biggest number is. But it is a very, very big number. So

Luke was more nearly right than you thought, wasn't he?"

Jeremy nodded.

"This reminds me of a verse in Proverbs," Mother said. "It says, 'Go not forth hastily to strive, lest thou know not what to do in the end thereof, when thy neighbour hath put thee to shame.' When we talk too quickly about things we really don't know about, then we will be ashamed when we find out the truth. If we aren't sure about something, it is better to check it out if we can, rather than to make a fuss about it."

"I will tell Luke tomorrow that we looked it up in the dictionary," Jeremy said. "I will tell him I'm sorry that I argued. How many zeroes did you say that number has, Mother?"

"One hundred," Mother answered. "Maybe Alice would like to write it on a piece of paper so that you can see what it looks like. I am glad you are willing to tell Luke that you are sorry. When we make a mistake, that is the right thing to do. That will help you to remember the next time you are tempted to argue about something you really don't know about."

"I know," Jeremy said. "I'll try to be more careful." He smiled at Mother and went to watch Alice write the number one googol on her paper.

When Alice was finished, she carried her paper to Mother. "This is what it looks like," she said. "I never knew there was such a big number."

"When people want to write this number, they often write it this way," Mother explained. She took Alice's pencil and wrote a big number 10 with a smaller number 100 beside it. "But I thought it would be good for you to write it the other way so we can see what a big number a googol really is. We all learned something new today, didn't we?"

Jeremy nodded and smiled. "Even you, Mother."

"Yes, even me," Mother agreed, returning Jeremy's smile. "We should never think we are too old to learn new things. Proverbs 1:5 says, 'A wise man will hear, and will increase learning.' I suppose that especially means that a wise man is willing to keep learning more about God and how to become more like God wants him to be. But there are also many other right and good things for us to learn, and we want to be willing to learn them too."

"Like the number one googol," Alice said.

"That's right," Mother agreed. "We don't ever want to become too proud to learn things from others. God is pleased when we have a heart that is willing to learn."

29.

A Good Example to Follow

"I'm tired of coloring," Timothy said as he put his brown crayon back into the box. He had just finished coloring a picture of a little boy who was feeding a flock of hens. "Let's do something else."

"I'm almost done with my picture too," Hannah answered, choosing a red crayon from the box. "Shall we play store when I'm finished?"

"Yes, let's," Timothy agreed. "May I be the clerk?"

"Yes, at least for a while," Hannah said. "I will have my house on the porch, and Sylvia can be my little girl. I will come and buy things from you. Let's have our store here in the living room."

Hannah and Timothy set up chairs for their shelves. They got toys out of the toy box and put them on the shelves. Two-year-old Sylvia helped too. She brought her toy duck and her doll to put in the store.

Hannah skipped to the kitchen. "Mother," she asked, "do you have anything that we may put in our store?"

Mother thought for a moment. "Oh, I just put an empty baking soda box in the wastebasket. And I think I threw a butter box away yesterday. Maybe I can still find it. And you may have the broom and the dustpan if you put them away when you are finished."

"We will," Hannah promised.

Mother found the butter box and the soda box. Hannah took them to the living room and set them neatly on a shelf. Then she returned for the broom and the dustpan. She placed them beside one of the shelves.

Mother came to the doorway. "You may have these grocery bags too," she said. "You might need them to put your groceries in. And here are some little bags. You could pretend that they have flour and sugar in them."

"Thank you, Mother." Hannah took the bags and laid them behind the counter.

"Now we are ready to start," she announced. "Come, Sylvia. Let's go to our house." She took Sylvia's hand and led her to the porch.

"Store?" Sylvia asked, looking back at Timothy.

"We will go to the store soon," Hannah promised. She took her little broom and swept the porch floor. Then she said, "Come, Sylvia. We will go to the store now."

Timothy, the "clerk," stood behind the counter. He had a little cardboard box for his cash register.

"I'm going to pretend that I'm that man we saw at the hardware store yesterday," Timothy announced.

"You mean the one with long hair?" Hannah asked in surprise.

Timothy nodded.

Hannah looked doubtful. "Why do you want to be that man?" she asked. "I don't think Mother would like that," she said. "Men are not supposed to have long hair."

"But why can't men have long hair?" Timothy asked. "Mothers and girls do."

"I don't know," Hannah answered. "But Father doesn't, and none of the other men at church do. And Mother gives you a haircut because you are a boy."

"Let's go ask Mother why men shouldn't have long hair," Timothy suggested.

Together Hannah and Timothy hurried out to the kitchen. Sylvia toddled behind them.

"Mother," Hannah began, "why doesn't Father have long hair?"

"I wanted to be that man we saw in the store yesterday," Timothy explained. "But Hannah said I shouldn't. She said men shouldn't have long hair."

"Hannah is right," Mother said. "Hannah, please go and get my Bible."

Hannah went to the living room and soon returned with Mother's Bible. Mother opened it to 1 Corinthians 11. She read verse 14 and part of verse 15. "'Doth not even nature itself teach you, that, if a man have long hair, it is a shame unto him? But if a woman have long hair, it is a glory to her.'

"These verses teach us that it is shameful for a man to have long hair," Mother explained.

"But God wants women to have long hair. That is God's plan. We want to follow God's plan."

"I didn't know the Bible says that," Timothy said soberly. "I don't want to be that man in the store after all. Why did he have long hair, Mother?"

"Maybe he never read the Bible to know what it says," Mother said. "Or maybe he doesn't want to obey the Bible. Some people think that their own way will make them happier than following the Bible. But that is never true. God is not pleased when we think our own way is best."

"I want to obey the Bible," Hannah said.

"So do I," Timothy agreed.

"So do I," Sylvia repeated.

Mother smiled at her. "I am glad all of my children want to obey God. God loves little children, and He wants all of them to grow up to live for Him.

"And, Timothy," Mother said, "if you want to pretend, I want you to pretend to be someone who obeys the Bible. People who love and obey God are good examples for us to follow."

Timothy thought for a moment. "I know. I'll be Brother Dale. He has a store, and he obeys God, doesn't he, Mother?"

"He surely does," Mother agreed. "You may

pretend that you are Brother Dale. Brother Dale is a good example."

Timothy and Hannah went back to their play in the living room.

"Brother Dale," Hannah asked, "may I buy some flour?" She giggled.

Timothy tried to look grown up. "Yes, here it is." He picked up a bag of pretend flour and smiled at Hannah. "That is two dollars."

"Thank you," Hannah said. "I want a box of butter and a doll for my little girl too." She picked up the butter and Sylvia's doll.

"That will be six dollars," Timothy said. He put the butter and the flour into a bag. He gave the doll to Sylvia.

Hannah pretended to pay Timothy. Then she took Sylvia's hand, and they walked out of the store.

Timothy watched Hannah go back to her pretend house. He was happy because he was obeying Mother. He knew that he was doing right by pretending to be someone who loved and obeyed God.

30.

The Borrowed Dollar

"Beth! Rosie!" Mother called to the twins from the kitchen window. "Come and put clean dresses on. I am going to K-Mart to pick up the bookcase that Father ordered. You may go with me if you come right away."

Beth and Rosie quickly dropped their sand shovels and hurried to the house. It did not take them long to change their dresses. Mother quickly combed their hair.

"May we take the money along that we got from Grandmother for our birthdays, Mother?"

Beth asked. "We haven't spent it yet."

"Yes, you may take it along," Mother answered.

Beth and Rosie ran to their bedroom for the five-dollar bills Grandmother had given them for their birthdays. Mother got the diaper bag and picked up baby Carol.

"Okay, are we ready to go?" Mother asked.

"I am." Rosie headed toward the door, and Beth followed. Mother came last, and she closed and locked the door.

Rosie wiggled excitedly on the car seat as they drove along. "I can hardly wait!" she said over and over. "Please hurry, Mother."

Mother laughed. "Calm down, dear," she said. "We will get there soon enough."

They drove for ten miles; then Rosie saw the big sign that said, "Welcome to Bloomfield." Soon they drove up to the big K-Mart store, and Mother parked the car in a parking space.

Rosie reached into her pocket to make sure her money was still there. Then she followed Mother and Beth into the store.

The girls followed Mother around as she did her shopping. Rosie watched her put a bottle of dish detergent, a pack of pens, and some batteries for the flashlight into her cart.

"Where is the bookcase?" Rosie wondered.

"I will ask someone to carry it to the cash register for me," Mother answered. "It's too heavy for me. But we want to get the other things we want first. Now what would you girls like to look at?"

"The games!" Rosie exclaimed at once.

"I think I would like to look at the notebooks and markers and things like that," Beth said.

"All right, we are close to the aisle where the school supplies are, so we will look at Beth's things first," Mother decided.

Beth took her time looking at the many pretty notebooks. She looked at the pens and the markers.

"I think I want this notebook," she said, picking up a pink one with a cute little kitten on it. "And this pack of ten markers."

"Is that all you want?" Mother asked.

"I think so," Beth answered. "How much will it cost?"

Mother figured quickly in her head. "One dollar and ninety-nine cents, with tax," she answered.

"Then I will have quite a bit left," Beth said. "I think I will save the rest now. Maybe another time I'll find something that I like very much."

"That's a good idea," Mother approved. "Okay, let's go look at the games now."

Mother and the girls walked over to the games together. Mother helped Rosie look over the games. Some of them were very silly, and Rosie knew she did not want them.

"Oh, Mother! Here is a Memory game! Lucy has one like this. It's lots of fun, and it's something that Beth and I could play together. May I get it, Mother?"

Mother looked at the price. "Five dollars and sixty-six cents," she read. "But you only have five dollars, Rosie. This will be six dollars with tax."

"But I could borrow a dollar from Beth," Rosie suggested. "She will have some left over, you said. I still have those two half-dollars at home that Mrs. Miller gave me for helping her weed her flowers. May I, Mother?"

Mother looked thoughtful. "I guess you may," she said, "if it is all right with Beth."

"Yes, that's okay," Beth said.

Ten minutes later, Rosie happily carried her treasure to the car. Beth followed, with her notebook and markers in a small paper bag. Behind her came Mother and a man who was

carrying the box that had the parts for the bookcase in it.

Mother opened the back door of the station wagon, and the man put the box inside.

"Thank you," Mother said.

"You're welcome," the man replied. Then he walked back to the store.

When they arrived home, Rosie carried the game upstairs and laid it on her bed. She carefully opened the plastic wrap around it and opened the box. She took out all the cards and looked at their shiny newness.

"I wish I wouldn't have to pay Beth back," she thought. "I would like to keep those half-dollars. They look so shiny and new. Maybe Beth will forget that I borrowed money from her. I just won't say anything about it."

"Rosie, time to set the table for supper!" Beth called up the stairs.

Rosie quickly put everything back into the box. She closed the box and put it into her drawer. Then she went downstairs to help Mother.

"Don't forget to pay back the money you borrowed from me," Beth whispered to Rosie as Rosie took the plates from the cupboard. Rosie did not say anything. She carried the stack of plates over to the table and put one at each person's place.

Beth did not say any more about the dollar that evening. "Maybe she forgot about it," Rosie thought hopefully.

The next morning the family had breakfast and family worship. When Rosie was finished washing the dishes, Mother said, "Rosie, please watch baby Carol for me while I go outside and pick the tomatoes."

Beth was still drying dishes. Rosie sat down on the floor and rolled the ball to baby Carol. Soon Beth was finished, and she came into the living room.

"Don't forget, Rosie," she reminded. "You still didn't give me that dollar."

"Can't you see that I'm busy?" Rosie snapped.

Beth looked hurt. She walked slowly out to the kitchen. Rosie heard the kitchen door open and close.

"Oh, I shouldn't have snapped at her like that," Rosie thought. "What if she goes and tells Mother?"

Ten minutes later, Mother came in from the garden. She washed her hands at the sink, and then she came into the living room.

"Rosie," she said, "did you give Beth her dollar back that you borrowed from her yesterday?"

"No, I didn't," Rosie answered. "She always asks me when I'm busy."

"Why did you snap at her just now?" Mother wanted to know.

Rosie hung her head. "I—I—" How foolish it sounded to say it! "I was hoping she would forget about it, and then I wouldn't have to pay it."

A sad look came over Mother's face. "Do you think that was right, Rosie?"

Rosie shook her head. She did not look up at Mother.

"Rosie, the Bible says, 'The wicked borroweth, and payeth not again: but the righteous sheweth mercy, and giveth.' God's people would rather lend something, if they can, than borrow something. But sometimes we do need to borrow something. If we do, we must try to return it or pay it back as soon as possible. Do you understand?"

Rosie nodded slowly.

"You are really stealing from Beth if you do not return her money," Mother continued. "Stealing is taking from another person what belongs to him. That dollar belongs to Beth, and you need to give it to her. It is also lying when we make a promise and don't keep it. You promised Beth that you would pay her back."

"I didn't know that I was stealing," Rosie said soberly. "I don't want to steal, and I don't want to tell a lie either."

"You did not need to give Beth the money when you were doing a job I had told you to do," Mother said. "But you should have told Beth that you will get it as soon as you can, and then you should have done it. What are you going to do now, Rosie?"

"May I go and get the money for her right now?" Rosie asked. "And I will tell her I am sorry for snapping at her."

"Yes, you may go," Mother answered. "I am glad you want to do it right away. God always blesses those who honor and obey His Word."

31.

God's Wonderful Plan

"Let's play something else, Dale," Elsie said. "We've been playing with our Play-Doh for a long time."

"All right," Dale agreed. He picked up the little pigs and the fence he had made and flattened them before putting them back into the Play-Doh container. "What shall we play?"

"Let's play church," Elsie suggested.

"Okay," Dale agreed. "I'll go wash my hands. Then I'll get Teddy and your two dolls."

"Okay," Elsie answered. "I'll get the

songbooks and put the Play-Doh away."

Soon Dale came with the dolls and Teddy. He gave the dolls to Elsie and sat down with Teddy beside him.

"You can be the preacher, Dale," Elsie said. She set her big doll on the step beside her and her little doll on her lap.

"Why do I always have to be the preacher?" Dale asked. "Why can't you preach this time?"

"Because women don't preach," Elsie explained.

"Why don't they?" Dale wanted to know.

Elsie thought for a moment. "I don't know, really," she said. "I just know that they don't. Let's go ask Mother. I think she's out in the garden."

Elsie and Dale ran out to the garden, but they stopped when they saw a green car parked in the lane. It was their neighbor, Mrs. Jones, and she was talking to Mother.

"We had such a good sermon yesterday," Mrs. Jones was saying. "Our new pastor, Mrs. Conley, is an excellent speaker. She knows her Bible very well. I like her better than Mr. Lawson, our last preacher."

Dale's eyes got big, and he looked at Elsie with questions in his eyes. Elsie shook her head

and put her finger to her lips. "Come, let's go back to the house," she said. "We will ask Mother later."

The children hurried back to the house. Elsie sat down with her dolls, and Dale announced, "Let's sing first."

Together they sang, "'This little light of mine, / I'm going to let it shine; / This little light of mine, / I'm going to let it shine, / Let it shine, let it shine let it shine. . . .'"

A few minutes later, Mother came into the house. "Did you children want something when Mrs. Jones was here?" she asked as she came to the stair door. "Oh, I'm sorry. I didn't mean to interrupt your church service."

"We were going to ask you a question," Elsie said. "I told Dale he can be the preacher, and he asked why I can't preach. I said women don't preach. But why don't they, Mother?"

"And, Mother, I heard Mrs. Jones say that their preacher's name is Mrs. Conley. That's a lady, isn't it?" Dale added.

"Yes, Dale, that is a lady." Mother answered Dale's question first. "Elsie, please go and get my Bible from my nightstand."

Elsie hurried to obey. Soon she returned, carefully carrying Mother's Bible.

Mother opened her Bible to 1 Corinthians 14. "This verse says, 'Let your women keep silence in the churches,'" Mother explained, pointing to the verse she was talking about. "There is also another verse that says, 'Let the woman learn in silence.' When you are older, you will understand some of these things better. God has a plan for everyone. He has a plan for men and a plan for women and a plan for children. God wants men to be the ones who preach at church. He wants women and children to listen and learn. God's plan is a wonderful plan.

"Now, you wondered about Mrs. Jones's preacher," Mother said. Her face was sober. "Mrs. Jones tried to tell me that God didn't really mean that women may not preach. But we still believe that God means just what He said. We must believe and obey the Bible even when others don't."

"That's why you wear a covering too, isn't it, Mother?" Elsie asked. "You said one time that you wear a covering because you want to follow God's plan."

"Yes, that is right," Mother agreed. "God has planned that men shall be the heads of their homes. God wants women to obey their husbands, and He wants them to wear a covering to show that they are following God's plan."

"And God wants children to obey their mothers and fathers, doesn't He?" Dale asked.

"That's right," Mother agreed. "That is all part of God's plan. Many people in the world want to follow their own plan instead of God's. But only those who follow God's plan are true

Christians. They are the only ones who are truly happy."

"We want to follow God's plan, don't we, Mother?" Elsie asked.

"Yes, that is right," Mother agreed. "We always want to obey what God says in His Word."

"I want to follow God's plan too," Dale said. "Come, Elsie. Let's play. And I'm going to be the preacher!"

"Let's sing 'The B-I-B-L-E' together first," Mother suggested, smiling at the children.

Joyfully the children sang with Mother, "'The B-I-B-L-E, / Yes, that's the Book for me; / I stand alone on the Word of God, / The B-I-B-L-E.'"

"Why did you want to sing that song, Mother?" Elsie asked when they were finished.

"Because that song is about the Bible," Mother explained. "The Bible is the Word of God, and it teaches us how to live the way God wants us to. The Bible is the most precious book in all the world, and we want to treasure it and obey it." Mother closed her Bible gently and rubbed her hand over its cover.

"I am glad God gave us the Bible," Elsie said. "I like to learn about God."

"That is good," Mother said. "I hope you will

always want to obey God and His Word. The Bible tells us how to please God. When we obey God all the time because it is right, then we are truly happy."

32.

God Made Mothers Special

"Put your books away. It's time to go home," Sister Edna announced.

Eldon closed his reading book and put it into his desk. He stood with the others to sing the closing song. Then Sister Edna dismissed them.

"Come on, Eldon," his older sister Rachel called when he stepped outside the schoolhouse. "We're ready to go!" She and Eleanor were already starting out the school lane.

Eldon hurried to catch up with his sisters.

As they started down the road, he swung his lunch box back and forth. "Let's play ball when we get home," he suggested.

"You know we can't play when we get home," Rachel reminded him. "We girls will have wash to fold, and there might be work in the garden to do too. And Father will probably need you to help him."

"I know," Eldon said. "It's not fair that we always have to work when we get home."

"Don't complain, Eldon," Rachel said. "You know what your memory verse for Sunday school was a few weeks ago: 'Work with your own hands.'"

"Yes, but do you know what our neighbor boy, Leonard, told me?" Eldon asked. "He said that his mother works in a factory, and when he comes home from school, she isn't even there. He doesn't have to do any work; he can do whatever he wants to. That sounds like that would be fun!"

Eleanor disagreed. "I don't think so. Eldon, do you really think you'd like to come home from school if Mother wasn't there? Leonard doesn't even have any brothers or sisters to play with, or anyone to talk to until his parents come home. I wouldn't like that at all!"

"I still think that would be more fun than working as soon as we get home," Eldon said. "I could find lots of things to do."

They reached the house, and Eldon flung the screen door open. The house was very quiet. "Mother!" Eldon called. There was no answer.

"Oh, here is a note," Rachel noticed. She picked it up from the table.

Mrs. Boyd fell and hurt her leg. Father and I are taking her to the hospital. If we are not home when you get here, you may have a snack of cookies and milk. You may play or do whatever you like until we get home. If you need help, go to Grand-mother's trailer.

Love,
Mother

"Now we can play ball if you want to, Eldon," Rachel said as she poured milk into a glass for him.

"Oh, yes, let's!" Eldon exclaimed.

After changing their clothes, the children played ball for a little while. But soon Eldon walked over to the maple tree and plopped down under it. "I'm tired of playing ball," he said. Rachel and Eleanor joined him.

"It just doesn't seem right without Mother here," Eldon said. "I don't even feel like playing. I wish they would hurry and come home."

"I do too," Eleanor agreed.

Suddenly Rachel began to laugh.

"What's so funny?" Eldon demanded.

"Well, just a little while ago you were complaining that you have to work when you get home," Rachel said. "You wished you'd have it like Leonard. And now Mother is gone just one time, and you don't even feel like playing. And you aren't even alone like Leonard is, because Eleanor and I are here too."

Eldon began to grin too. "I guess that is funny, isn't it? Well, even if it is, I do wish Mother would come."

"I agree with you. I want her to come soon too," Rachel told him.

"I wonder if Mother has any wash for us to fold," Eleanor said. "That's usually our job when we get home from school on Thursdays. I'm going to go in and see."

"May I help too?" Eldon asked.

"Of course," Eleanor answered. "Come on!" They dashed to the house.

Eleanor found two basketfuls of laundry in

Mother's bedroom. She and Eldon carried them out to the living room. "You may fold the washcloths and the handkerchiefs," Eleanor offered. "They are the easiest things."

"It's almost time to make supper," Rachel said. "I know how to make tomato soup and grilled cheese sandwiches. Maybe we can have supper ready when they come home."

When Eldon and Eleanor had finished folding the wash, Eldon asked, "What can we do now?"

"You may set the table while Eleanor and I put the wash away," Rachel suggested.

Eldon sang, "'Jesus loves me! This I know, / For the Bible tells me so'" as he neatly set the table. His sisters joined in too: "'Little ones to Him belong; / They are weak but He is strong. . . .'"

The children had such fun working on their surprises that the time passed quickly. It was almost five-thirty when they heard the car drive in the lane.

"Why, what do we have here?" Mother exclaimed as she entered the kitchen. "Something smells very good."

"Rachel made supper," Eldon told her quickly. "And Eleanor and I—"

272

"Sh-h! Don't tell!" Eleanor put her hand on Eldon's mouth. "Let Mother find out herself."

Mother smiled. "Well, there must be another surprise somewhere. I guess I'll have to go look for it. I wonder where I should look. I'll put my coat away first."

Mother went to her bedroom to put her coat away. When she came out, she was smiling. "Did I leave two empty clothes baskets in my room?" she asked, her eyes twinkling.

"We folded the wash for you!" Eldon clapped his hands with excitement. "I folded the hand-kerchiefs and the washcloths, and Eleanor did the other things."

"Thank you very much, children," Mother said. "It is very nice to come home and find supper all ready and the wash folded."

"Mother, on the way home from school Eldon said that he wished he wouldn't have to work. He wished he could come home and play like Leonard can," Rachel said. "You know, Leonard is all alone after school until his mother comes home from work."

"But, Mother, that wasn't so much fun after all," Eldon said sheepishly. "I didn't like com-ing home to such a quiet house and eating our snack without you here. We couldn't tell you what happened at school. It wasn't even fun to play. It was lots more fun to be helpers and surprise you."

"I think this was a good lesson for you, Eldon," Mother said. "God planned for families. It is Father's job to earn money so that we can buy the things we need. The Bible says that mothers should be 'keepers at home.' That means a mother should stay at home and take care of the children and the house. God wants children to be obedient and to be helpers. We are happy when we follow God's plan."

"God wants mothers to make our homes happy places, where we like to come," Father added. "I don't like to come into the quiet house when Mother is away. It doesn't seem right at all. I guess I'm just like Eldon." He laid his hand on Eldon's shoulder. "God gave mothers a very special place in the family. We are thankful for Mother, aren't we?"

All the children nodded vigorously.

"I am glad that our family follows God's plan," Eldon said, looking at his happy family. "I won't complain about my work after this."

"Good," Father said, giving Eldon a special smile.

33.

Dorcas's Reward

"Mother, when is Sister Amy coming?" Dorcas asked. She came to stand beside Mother, who was feeding baby Michael.

"She will come in about one hour," Mother answered with a smile. "You like it when Sister Amy comes, don't you?"

"Yes." Dorcas's eyes sparkled. "I like it when she comes and brings our supper. Last time she brought a peanut butter pie. That was yummy!" Dorcas went to the window and looked out. She wished that Sister Amy would come right now.

"Why don't you color a picture in your coloring book," Mother suggested. "The time will pass more quickly if you are busy."

Dorcas turned away from the window. She had an idea. "Mother, may I draw a picture for Sister Amy and color it?" she asked.

"Yes, you may," Mother answered. "That would be very nice."

Dorcas found a piece of paper and a pencil. She sat down at the table and began to draw a picture of a little girl who was picking flowers.

When she was done coloring her picture, Mother said, "Dorcas, will you please keep Michael happy while I finish putting the laundry away?"

"Okay." Dorcas put her crayons and her pencil away. She laid the picture on Father's desk. Then she skipped to Mother.

"Mother, may I hold Michael on the porch swing?" Dorcas asked. "He likes that. Then I can see when Sister Amy comes."

"That would be fine," Mother agreed. "I'll carry Michael outside and put him on your lap. Hold him carefully."

Dorcas was sitting on the porch swing with her little brother when a blue car drove in the

lane a while later. "She's here, Mother!" Dorcas cried.

Michael squealed and gurgled, waving his arms excitedly.

Sister Amy got out of her car and opened the back door. She took out a box and came up the walk with it.

"What do you have in there?" Dorcas asked eagerly. She knew it was something for their supper.

"It's a tomato salad and a tuna and noodle casserole," Sister Amy answered. "Do you like that?"

"Oh, yes!" Dorcas answered. "We don't have tuna and noodle casserole very often."

"And I made apple crunch for dessert," Sister Amy said. "Your mother said she has ice cream in the freezer that we can eat with it."

"Oh, good!" Dorcas said happily.

Sister Amy carried the box into the house. Then she came outside to Dorcas and Michael again. "Shall I take Michael?" she asked.

"Sure." Dorcas let go of her little brother as he reached for Sister Amy. He knew Sister Amy, and he liked it when she held him.

Dorcas hopped off the swing and took Sister Amy's hand, and they went into the house.

Mother was setting the table.

"Can I help you with something?" Sister Amy asked Mother.

"It's okay if you just keep the children entertained until we're ready to eat," Mother answered. "Benjamin said he will be in around six-thirty." Benjamin was Dorcas's father.

"Shall we read a story?" Sister Amy asked.

"Yes!" Dorcas hurried to the bookcase to get the book *Molly Helps Mother.* She sat down and laid her head on Sister Amy's shoulder as Sister Amy began to read.

Soon Father came in, and everyone sat down to enjoy the delicious supper. Dorcas liked Sister Amy's casserole, and she took a second helping.

When supper was over, Sister Amy began to wash the dishes. Dorcas picked up a tea towel and began to dry them carefully.

"Sister Amy, where do you live?" Dorcas asked.

"It is about six miles from your house to the place where I live," Sister Amy answered. "Do you know where Harlan and Beth live? I live close to their house."

"Yes, I know where they live," Dorcas said. Her forehead puckered up in a puzzled frown.

"Do you live all by yourself?"

"No," Sister Amy answered as she placed another plate on the drainer. "I live with an old man named Richard and an old lady named Hannah. They cannot do much work anymore, and they need someone to take care of them."

"I don't think I know them," Dorcas said slowly.

"No, I don't think you do," Sister Amy answered. "They go to a different church than we do. Sometimes they can't go to church at all because they don't feel well."

"Don't you have any little children at your house?" Dorcas asked.

"No, we don't," Sister Amy answered, giving Dorcas a smile.

"Why don't you?" Dorcas looked up into Sister Amy's face. "You don't have a father either, do you? Why do you just live with an old man and an old lady?"

Sister Amy smiled kindly into Dorcas's puzzled face. "I live with them because that is what God wants me to do," she explained. "God planned for your mother and father to get married and have you and Michael to take care of.

"But He had a different plan for me. I don't know if He will want me to have a husband and little children someday or not, but for now He hasn't given me any. Richard and Hannah need someone to care for them, and God gave me that job to do. We are always happy when we obey God, whatever His will is for us. Always remember that, Dorcas."

"Mother told me that too," Dorcas said. "One time I wanted to help Mother peel peaches. But she said I was too little. She said that if I kept Michael happy, that would be helping her a lot. She said that some work is for fathers to do and some is for mothers and some is for children. God planned that we should help each other, and we are happy when we follow God's plan."

"And you were, weren't you?" Sister Amy asked.

"Yes." Dorcas nodded her head. "I wanted to peel peaches, but I obeyed Mother and took care of Michael. It made me happy to do what Mother said."

"Mother," Dorcas asked when the dishes were done, "may I give Sister Amy a piece of the candy that Father got today?"

"Why, yes, you may," Mother answered. "It's

in a bag in the corner cupboard. Maybe Sister Amy can reach it for you."

Sister Amy got the bag and handed it to Dorcas. Dorcas opened it and took out a tiny chocolate bar. "This is for you," she said, laying it in Sister Amy's hand.

"M-m-m. Chocolate! That is my favorite kind," Sister Amy said.

Dorcas beamed. She was getting ready to close the bag again when she thought of something. "Mother, may I give Sister Amy two more pieces? The old man and lady she lives with might like to have some too."

"Yes, that would be very nice," Mother agreed.

"Here is one for . . . for Hannah," Dorcas said, laying another piece in Sister Amy's hand. "And this one is for Richard."

"Okay," Sister Amy answered. "I will give the candy to them. Thank you, Dorcas."

"You're welcome," Dorcas said. She closed the bag and gave it to Sister Amy to put back in its place.

"I made a picture for you," Dorcas said. "Do you want to see it?"

"Certainly," Sister Amy answered. "Where is it?"

"It's on Father's desk in the living room," Dorcas answered.

Sister Amy followed Dorcas into the living room.

"Here it is," Dorcas said, handing the picture to Sister Amy.

"What a nice picture," Sister Amy said admiringly. "Is this little girl you?"

"Yes, and I'm picking flowers for you," Dorcas said.

"Well, isn't that nice." Sister Amy smiled and gave Dorcas a hug. "Thank you very much."

"You're welcome," Dorcas answered.

Dorcas was quiet for a few moments.

"What are you thinking?" Sister Amy asked.

"Oh, I'd like to give something for your old lady too," Dorcas said. "Would she like a picture?"

"I'm sure she would," Sister Amy answered.

"I can draw one right now," Dorcas decided.

Dorcas sat down at the table. Carefully she began to draw.

"What are you making?" Sister Amy asked.

"I'm making an old lady in a rocking chair," Dorcas told her. When she was done drawing, she got her crayons to color her picture.

"What color shall I make her dress?" she asked Sister Amy.

"Well . . ." Sister Amy thought a moment. "Hannah has a green dress that she wears at home a lot."

"Then I will make her dress green," Dorcas decided. She pulled her green crayon out of the box.

When Dorcas had finished her picture, she gave it to Sister Amy.

"Thank you, Dorcas," Amy said. "I think Hannah will like your picture very much."

All too soon for Dorcas, it was time for Sister Amy to leave. Dorcas followed Sister Amy out to her car. "Will you come to our house again sometime?" she asked.

"Oh, I would like to," Sister Amy answered. "I like to come to your house because I don't have any little children at my house."

Dorcas smiled. "You can talk to me at my house, and you can hold Michael," she said.

"That's right," Sister Amy agreed. "Good-bye now."

"Good-bye." Dorcas waved as Sister Amy drove out the lane. Then she ran to the house.

Several weeks later Sister Amy talked to Dorcas's mother after prayer meeting. "May

Dorcas come out to my car with me?" she asked. "I have a surprise for her."

"Yes, she may go," Mother answered while smiling at Dorcas.

Dorcas put her hand in Sister Amy's and went out to the car with her. Sister Amy took a little paper bag from the front seat of her car and handed it to Dorcas.

"What is it?" Dorcas asked.

"Open it and see," Sister Amy answered with a twinkle in her eyes.

Dorcas opened the bag and pulled something out. "Oh, what is it? Is it a doll quilt?" she asked, her eyes shining.

"Yes, it is," Sister Amy answered. "It's from Hannah. She made it for you."

"Oh, it is pretty." Dorcas rubbed her fingers over the material. "Can you tell her 'thank you' for me?"

"I will do that," Sister Amy agreed. "Do you know why she gave you this doll quilt?"

Dorcas shook her head.

"She was happy for the candy you gave her and for the picture you drew for her," Sister Amy said. "She put your picture on the refrigerator door. Last week she was sewing a quilt, and she had some patches left over. She said she wanted to make a doll quilt for the little girl who drew that picture for her."

Dorcas giggled. "That was me."

Sister Amy smiled. "Yes, it was," she said.

"I will put it in our car," Dorcas decided. "Then I will show Mother on the way home."

Before long it was time to go home. "Oh, Mother, see my doll quilt?" Dorcas held it up for Mother to see as they rode in the car.

Mother turned around and looked at the quilt. "That is very pretty," she agreed. "You can use that in your little cradle."

"The old lady that lives with Sister Amy gave it to me," Dorcas explained. "She liked the candy and the picture I made for her. Now I am glad that I gave her those things."

"It was very nice of Hannah to give you that quilt," Father said as he drove. "But remember that we don't do nice things for others only to receive something for ourselves. We do kind things because we know that is what Jesus wants us to do."

"Old people often get very lonely," Mother added. "They enjoy it when little children do kind things for them. That makes them very happy."

"I will try to remember to be kind all the

time, even if I don't get a gift," Dorcas decided. "But I am happy for my quilt too."

"That's the way to be," Father answered with a smile. "We don't do kind things only for the rewards we get. But God is pleased when we are thankful for the kind things that others do for us too."

34.

She Isn't Our Mother

"Richard, Nevin, it's time to get up," Father called, shaking the two boys gently.

Richard rolled over and opened his eyes. "Why is Father calling us?" he wondered sleepily. "Where is Mother?" It was usually Mother who called the boys when it was time for them to get up.

"Boys," Father said, "Mother is sick this morning. I must go to work, but Sister Sharon, your Sunday school teacher, will be coming. She will take care of you boys and baby Elsie and do the work that needs to be done."

Father left the room, and Richard and Nevin began to get dressed. Then they hurried downstairs. Father was at the sink peeling oranges.

"It's funny to see you making breakfast, Father," Richard laughed.

"It feels funny to me too." Father laughed with him. "I hope I can make a breakfast that is good enough."

"I think you can," Richard said. "But maybe not as good as Mother's."

"Father, can you tie my shoes, please?" Nevin asked.

"Surely," Father answered. "Wait till I'm finished peeling this orange; then I'll wash my hands and tie your shoes."

Soon Father and the boys were seated at the table. Father prayed, and then they began to eat.

"I don't like it without Mother at the table," Richard said. He pushed his oatmeal around and around in his bowl with his spoon.

"I think Mother will soon be feeling better," Father said comfortingly. "She just needs to rest. It doesn't seem right to me either when Mother isn't with us at the table. Mother helps to make our home a happy place, doesn't she?"

The boys nodded. Richard stopped stirring his oatmeal and put a spoonful in his mouth. He was glad that Father understood how he was feeling.

When breakfast was over, the boys helped Father with the dishes. They were almost finished when Father announced, "Sister Sharon is here."

Sister Sharon came up the walk, and Nevin opened the door for her. "Thank you," she said with a smile. She said hello to Father and Richard; then she went to the bedroom to talk to Mother.

Father took his coat from the hook in the closet and put it on. "Remember to be good for Sharon today," he reminded the boys. "When she tells you something, I expect you to obey her just like you would obey Mother."

Richard and Nevin nodded. Father gave them each a good-bye kiss; then he picked up his lunch pail and headed out the door.

After a while Sharon came out of the bedroom, carrying baby Elsie. When she had fed and dressed her, she asked the boys, "Shall we go upstairs and make your beds?"

Richard and Nevin followed Sister Sharon

upstairs. She went into the boys' room to make the bed and set Elsie on the floor to play with some toys.

Richard and Nevin stayed out in the hall to play. Just then Richard had a naughty idea. "Let's jump on the spare bed," he suggested to Nevin.

Nevin's eyes got big. "But Mother said we shouldn't," he objected.

"Mother is downstairs. She can't see us," Richard said. "And Sister Sharon isn't our mother. She won't spank us."

Richard opened the spare bedroom door, and he and Nevin slipped inside. Soon they were gleefully bouncing on the big spare bed.

Soon Sister Sharon came to the door. "Boys!" she exclaimed. "Get off the bed. I'm sure your mother doesn't let you do that."

Richard kept on jumping. Nevin looked at Richard, and he did not stop either.

"Boys, did you hear what I said?" Sister Sharon pulled the two boys off the bed and firmly led them toward the stairsteps. "Come, I'm ready to go downstairs now."

The two boys slowly followed her downstairs. While Sister Sharon straightened up the living room, Richard had another idea. He stood at the living room door and began to run. He jumped up on the couch and from the couch over onto the easy chair. Then he ran back to the door to start over again.

"Richard." Sister Sharon took his arm and held it tightly. "I want you to stop that. Does your mother let you do that?"

Richard shook his head, but his eyes danced with mischief.

"Richard," Mother called from the bedroom, "come here."

Richard walked over to the bedroom door.

"Are you being obedient, Richard?" Mother asked. Her voice was quiet, and she looked very pale. "I want you to obey Sister Sharon just as you would obey me. Do you hear?"

Richard nodded. He went back to the living room. But it just did not seem so important to be obedient when Mother was too sick to spank him. And he was sure that Sister Sharon would not punish him. Several more times that day he got into mischief, and often Nevin would follow his example.

When Father came home from work, he asked, "And how did my boys behave today?"

Sister Sharon looked at the boys. "They didn't obey very well," she said sadly. She told Father some of the things the boys had done. "I think Nevin was usually following Richard's example."

Richard looked down at the floor. Now he

felt afraid. He had not thought that Sister Sharon might tell Father about how naughty he was.

"Come with me to the study, Richard," Father said firmly.

Slowly Richard followed Father. Father shut the study door.

"Richard," Father said sadly, "I am disappointed in you. I trusted you to obey Sister Sharon. Instead, you not only disobeyed, but you were also a bad example to your brother. I told you this morning that I wanted you to obey her as you would obey Mother. I will have to spank you."

Richard started to cry. "I'm sorry, Father," he sobbed.

"I believe you are sorry," Father said. "But we must help you remember how important it is to always obey."

When the spanking was over, Father said, "Now I want you to tell Sister Sharon you are sorry too. Sharon will probably come again tomorrow, and I want to hear a better report when I come home from work tomorrow than I did today."

"I will try to do better, Father," Richard promised. He followed Father out of the study.

Sister Sharon was slicing bread at the kitchen counter. Richard walked over to her. "I—I'm sorry I disobeyed," he said in a low voice. "I will obey you tomorrow."

Sharon smiled at him. "Good," she said kindly. "Then you will be happy."

"Now, Richard, I want you to set the table for Sister Sharon while Nevin and I go to the study," Father said. "Sister Sharon can get the plates and glasses down for you."

Richard hummed softly to himself as he placed the plates on the table. He was happier than he had been all day. "Disobeying didn't make me happy at all," he thought. "Tomorrow I will obey even if Father and Mother can't see me. God sees me all the time."

The next morning Mother was feeling a little better. She came to the table for breakfast, but then she went back to bed again.

"Richard, I will let you clear the table while I put a load of wash in the washer," Sister Sharon said. "If there is anything that you can't put away, just set it on the corner of the table, and I will put it away after I've started the wash."

"Okay," Richard answered.

Sister Sharon went to the laundry room.

Richard looked at Nevin, who was playing with his truck on the floor. He picked up the water pitcher. "It would be fun to pour this water on Nevin's head," he thought, grinning mischievously. "Wouldn't that surprise him?"

Richard started toward Nevin with the water pitcher, but suddenly he remembered something. He remembered what had happened in the study the evening before.

"I don't want that to happen again," he thought. "I want Sister Sharon to tell Father that we were good today." Richard carried the pitcher of water to the sink and poured the water down the drain.

When the dishes were washed, they all went upstairs while Sharon made the beds.

"Let's jump on the bed again like we did yesterday," Nevin suggested.

Richard shook his head. "No," he said. "That was naughty. We want to be obedient for Sharon today."

Sharon heard what Richard said. She smiled at Richard. "I am glad to hear you saying that, Richard. If you keep on being obedient as you have been so far today, I will have a good report to give to your father this evening."

Richard smiled, and his heart glowed inside.

He was glad he was making Sister Sharon happy.

When Father came home that evening, Richard and Nevin ran outside to meet him.

"Father, we tried very hard today to obey Sister Sharon," Richard told Father. "This morning I thought it would be fun to pour water on Nevin's head, but then I remembered—" he looked sheepishly at Father—"I remembered last night, and I didn't do it."

"Very good," Father approved. "That sounds much better than yesterday. We will ask her what she has to say about it."

"How did the boys behave today?" Father asked as he entered the kitchen.

"They did very well," Sister Sharon said as she smiled at the boys. "I could tell that Richard was trying hard to be a good example for his younger brother."

Father laid his hand on Richard's shoulder. "The Bible says, 'A wise son maketh a glad father,'" he said. "Christian parents are happy when they see their children making wise choices. Learning to obey is an important part of being wise. And you feel much better than you did yesterday, don't you?"

Richard nodded as he looked up into Father's smiling face.

"Obedience is always the best way," Father said, "because it is right. And because we know that it is God's way, it also makes us happy."

35.

A Dollar to Disobey

Seven-year-old Mary Jane swirled her dish-towel around and around inside the shiny glass bowl. Then she set the bowl carefully on the counter.

"What are you going to do after the dishes are washed, Mother?" she asked.

Mother looked at baby Warren, who was sitting in his infant seat on the table. "Warren is ready for a nap, and I am tired too," she answered. "I believe I will take him and go lie down for an hour or so."

"May I go outside?" Mary Jane asked.

"Yes, I suppose so, if you stay in the yard," Mother answered.

Soon Mary Jane was done drying the dishes. She gave her dishtowel to Mother and hopped off her low stool. After carrying the stool to the closet where it belonged, she headed for the door.

"What shall I do first?" she wondered. She was not used to playing all by herself. Usually her brothers, Allen and Paul, were there to play with her, but they had gone to a farm sale with Father that day.

"I know what! I'll bring Betsy out here, and I'll make a house under the weeping willow tree," she decided. She headed for the house to get her doll.

Soon Mary Jane was busy preparing her little house. She was so busy that she did not notice the neighbor's big girl, Carolyn, standing at the fence until Carolyn said, "Hi. What are you doing?"

Mary Jane looked up, startled.

"Surprised you, didn't I?" Carolyn laughed.

Mary Jane nodded. Carolyn's family had not lived in that house for very long. She had never talked to Carolyn before. Was Carolyn

going to make fun of her house?

"I'm playing house," she answered.

"That looks like a nice house," Carolyn said. "And you have a cute doll. What is her name?"

"Betsy," Mary Jane told her. She felt better now because Carolyn had not laughed at her.

"I have a doll too," Carolyn told Mary Jane. "She is bigger than Betsy. I don't play with her anymore, but she sits in a chair in my room. Would you like to see her?"

"Oh, yes," Mary Jane answered.

"Come with me, and I will show her to you," Carolyn invited.

"Oh!" Mary Jane had thought that Carolyn would bring the doll for her to see. She looked down at Betsy, and then up at Carolyn. "Mother said I must stay in the yard."

"She won't care if you come over here for just a little bit," Carolyn coaxed. "It will only take two minutes."

Mary Jane shook her head slowly. "I don't think Mother would like that."

Carolyn looked at Mary Jane for a while. "I know what!" she exclaimed. "I will give you a dollar if you come over with me."

Mary Jane's eyes opened wide. A whole dollar! She had never had a whole dollar for her very own. "Maybe Mother won't care if I go over if I show her my dollar," she thought.

She walked around the fence that separated their yard from the neighbors'. Carolyn smiled and took her hand as they walked toward the house.

Mary Jane did not feel very happy. "What will Mother say?" she wondered. She was not so sure after all that Mother would be pleased.

"Where is your mother?" Mary Jane asked Carolyn as they entered the quiet house.

"Mother is at work," Carolyn answered. "Come, my room is down this hall." They walked down the hall, and Carolyn stopped in front of one of the doors. She opened it, and Mary Jane followed her inside.

"Here is my doll," Carolyn said as she picked up a big doll dressed in a lacy pink dress.

"She is pretty!" Mary Jane breathed. "May I hold her?"

"Sure." Carolyn handed the doll to Mary Jane. Mary Jane held her carefully and stroked her silky black hair.

"Would you like to wear a dress like that?" Carolyn asked. She opened her closet door and showed Mary Jane a pink dress. "Look at this. I used to wear this dress, and my doll was dressed just like me."

"I—I don't know," Mary Jane answered. "We don't wear dresses with lace and things like that."

"I know you don't," Carolyn answered. "But you would look pretty in that dress. I'd like to dress you up in it. Would you like that?"

"I don't know." Mary Jane looked down at the floor. She did not think Mother would like that. "But it would be fun to be dressed like Carolyn's doll," she thought.

"You'll let me help you, won't you?" Carolyn coaxed. She reached for Mary Jane's zipper.

"Ma-ary Jane! Ma-ary Ja-ane!" Both girls heard it at the same time.

"That's Mother calling. I have to go home." Mary Jane wiggled away from Carolyn's hand.

"You don't need to go yet," Carolyn coaxed again. "She doesn't know where you are. You can put the dress on for just five minutes. I want to take a picture of you."

"Let me go," Mary Jane pleaded. "I have to obey Mother."

Carolyn sighed. "All right. Maybe you can come over another day."

Mary Jane did not think she wanted to come over again—not without Mother. She was

getting scared. She could still hear Mother calling her name.

Carolyn took her hand again and led her to the door. "Now go," she said, giving Mary Jane a little shove.

Mary Jane could see Mother standing on the porch. As soon as Mary Jane stepped outside the door, Mother saw her. She stopped calling.

Mary Jane wanted to run fast to Mother. But she was scared. Was Mother going to punish her?

"Mary Jane!" Mother exclaimed when Mary Jane came up to the porch. "Why were you at the neighbors' house?"

Mary Jane looked down at her feet.

"Come inside," Mother said firmly. "I want to hear what happened."

Mother led Mary Jane to the sofa. Mary Jane started to cry.

"Now tell me about it," Mother said.

"Ca-Carolyn—" Mary Jane could hardly talk. She started again. "Carolyn wanted me to come over and look at her doll. I—I told her that you said I must stay in the yard. But—but she said that she would give me a dollar if I would come."

"And what did you do over there?" Mother asked.

Mary Jane saw that her face was sober. "I held Carolyn's doll," Mary Jane said. "It was a pretty doll. She was wearing a lacy dress. Then Carolyn wanted to dress me in a dress like that. She had one just like it that she used to wear. But then we heard you calling. She said I didn't have to come right away. She wanted me to put that dress on, and she wanted to take a picture of me with that pretty dress on. But I said I must obey you."

"I am glad you came when I called," Mother said seriously. "But you disobeyed me by going out of the yard. I must punish you for that." Mother led Mary Jane into the study.

Mary Jane started to cry again.

After the spanking, Mother drew Mary Jane close to her. "Mary Jane," she said, "disobedience is very, very serious. Carolyn was not helping you to be obedient. You should have obeyed Mother, not her."

"But, Mother," Mary Jane said, "she said she would give me a dollar. I thought I could give my dollar in the offering on Sunday—you know, for the poor people in Russia."

"And did she give you a dollar?" Mother

asked, looking soberly at Mary Jane.

Mary Jane shook her head. "She probably forgot because I had to hurry home."

"Maybe," Mother answered. "We don't know what Carolyn was thinking. But she may not even have planned to give you a dollar. What Carolyn did to you is called a bribe. To try to get you to do what she wanted you to do, she bribed you by telling you she would give you a dollar.

"Also," Mother continued, "the Bible says, 'Behold, to obey is better than sacrifice.' It is much better for you to obey Mother than for you to have a dollar to give in the offering because you disobeyed. Do you understand?"

Mary Jane nodded slowly. "I think so."

"I do not want to scare you," Mother said, "but sometimes older children or adults take little children away and do very bad things to them. I do not know if Carolyn is that kind of girl or not. But you must *never, never* go with Carolyn or anyone else you do not know well, unless Father or I or another adult that you know says you may."

Mary Jane looked scared. "I didn't know that," she said. "I won't go with her again."

"We must always trust God to take care of

us," Mother said, putting her arm around Mary Jane's shoulders. "You do not need to be afraid every time you see a stranger. God sees us all the time, and He takes care of us. But it is very, very important for children to obey their parents. That is part of being safe too."

Mary Jane nodded soberly.

Several days later Mary Jane was outside on the swing. Carolyn came to the fence and watched for a while. "Come over and play on our swing," she invited. "It's on the other side of the house. It's a big swing, and it has a sliding board too. It has a playhouse at the top of the sliding board."

Mary Jane shook her head. "Mother said I'm not allowed to."

"Please," Carolyn begged. "I'll give you a dollar. I forgot the last time."

"No," Mary Jane said. "God wants me to obey Mother."

"Nothing will hurt you over here," Carolyn said. "Are you scared?"

Just then Mother stepped out onto the porch. "Mary Jane, will you please come in and rock Warren? He's getting sleepy."

Mary Jane hopped off the swing. As she walked to the house, she glanced over at

Carolyn. Carolyn had a scowl on her face. Mary Jane saw her turn around and head toward her house.

"I am so glad you obeyed, Mary Jane," Mother said as Mary Jane entered the kitchen. "I am sure Carolyn is very lonely while her parents are at work. We must pray for her and ask God to show us ways to be kind to her. But it is still important for you to obey and stay on our side of the fence."

Mary Jane nodded as she took Warren from his infant seat. "I feel so much better this time," she said. "I was afraid the other time because I didn't really think you would like it."

"We are always happy when we obey because it is God's way," Mother told her.

36.

At the Indian Museum

"Children, how would you like to go to the Indian museum tomorrow?" Father asked at the breakfast table one morning.

"Yes! Yes!" Matthew clapped his hands. Clara and Marcus looked happy too.

"I would enjoy that," big sister Dorcas said. "We've never been there."

"School will start in two weeks," Father said. "You children have been good helpers this summer, and we would like to do something special before school starts. Mother and

I have decided that it would be nice to take the family to the museum tomorrow morning and have a picnic lunch at a park close to the museum. Then in the afternoon we'd like to shop for school supplies and a few other things."

"If we want to do that, I need some good helpers today," Mother said. "I saw yesterday that there's quite a bit of corn that is ready to freeze. We should do it today. If Matthew and Clara will wash the dishes, Dorcas and I can go out and start picking corn. Marcus, you come out and carry our full baskets to the truck and bring us the empty ones again."

"I'll wash the dishes," Clara said.

"And I'll dry them," Matthew added.

The busy day passed quickly, and soon it was bedtime. Matthew was so excited about the next day that he could hardly relax in bed. But finally he fell asleep.

The next morning soon after breakfast, the Weiler family was on their way. After driving for about an hour, they arrived at the museum.

"Welcome to the Indian museum," said a man as they entered the big stone building. "I'll be ready to start a tour in about five minutes."

315

"All right," Father answered. "We'll just look around for a few minutes."

The family looked at some of the displays nearby while they waited for the group to gather. Soon the guide was ready to begin.

"These are stones that the Indians used for knives," the guide explained, pointing to several stones that lay on a table. "And these sharp bones were their needles." He explained a bit more about how the Indians used the knives and the needles. He showed them many other interesting things too.

"Here is a picture of an Indian riding a horse," the guide continued. He pointed with his stick to a large painting on the wall. "Horses were very useful to man, especially before the time of cars and trucks.

"By looking at old bones, men who study prehistoric life have figured out how horses evolved. A lot of bones were found in a cave about fifty miles from here. They are believed to be the bones of an animal that lived fifty million years ago, which evolved into the horse as we know it today."

Matthew tugged on Father's arm. "Father, what does *evolved* mean?" he whispered when Father looked down at him.

"We'll talk about it when we get out to the car," Father whispered back.

An hour later the tour was finished. "Thank you," Father said to the guide. The family walked out to the car.

When everyone was settled and they were on their way to the park, Father said, "Matthew, you asked me what *evolved* means. I should have explained something to you children before we went to the museum. But since I didn't, we'll talk about it now. Dorcas, do you know what *evolved* means?"

"Some people believe that the world started from a little dot and kept getting bigger and bigger. Or they think that animals came from a different kind of animal, or people came from monkeys," big sister Dorcas answered. "Instead of saying that God created the world and the animals and things, they say that things *evolved*. But it's not true, because the Bible says that God made the world and people and animals in six days."

"That's right," Father agreed. "The people Dorcas was telling us about believe that animals and people and other things just slowly became better. That is called evolution. But Christians know that God created the world according to His own plan. Apparently that guide is not a Christian. He told us many things that were true about the Indians. But what he said about things that evolved, such as the horse, was not true. Mother, did you hear anything else that wasn't true?"

"Yes," Mother answered. "Several times he told us about things that supposedly happened millions of years ago. But the Bible and Bible history teach us that the world is only about six thousand years old."

"A million is more than six thousand, isn't it?" Matthew asked.

"Yes, it is," Father answered. "A lot more. Another thing that I noticed was that when he was talking about the horse, he mentioned the term *prehistoric life. Prehistoric* means something that happened before the time that man knows about or has written about. According to the Bible, we do not believe that there was any life on the earth before God formed the world. And we have the Creation story in Genesis 1. We know that God lived before that, but all life on the earth was created at the time of Genesis 1."

"So you mean there isn't anything like prehistoric life, except for God?" Dorcas asked.

"That's right," Father agreed. "We hope you children enjoyed our visit to the museum," he continued. "We can learn a lot by visiting places like that and seeing how people used to live. But we need to remember that when people aren't Christians, they believe some things that aren't true. We must always believe and obey the Bible."

"Some teachers even teach their school-children that evolution is true," Dorcas said.

"Yes," Father answered sadly. "In many schools children are taught evolution. Many teachers do not believe what the Bible says about how God made the world. And some-times the teachers who do believe the Creation story aren't allowed to teach it to the children. God is not pleased when grownups teach chil-dren things that are not true."

"I am glad we go to a Christian school," Clara said. "I'm glad we learn true things."

"Yes, we should thank God often for our Christian school," Mother said.

"And any time you children have questions or don't know if something is true or not, ask Father or me, or someone else who is a Christ-ian," Mother added. "Matthew did the right thing when he asked Father about the word *evolved*."

"I'm glad I asked about that word," Matthew said. "I don't want to believe something that isn't true."

"I'm glad we have the Bible so that we can know what is true," Dorcas said.

"So am I," Matthew said, and Clara and Marcus nodded their heads.

"We are always safe when we believe the Bible and obey it," Father finished as he drove the car into a parking space at the park.

37.

Sandra and Santa Claus

"What are you going to get here, Mother?" Sandra asked as Mother pulled into the parking lot of the department store.

"I want to get a pair of slippers for Grandmother," Mother answered. "And Father wants me to look for a screwdriver. He broke his yesterday."

Sandra climbed out of the car and took Mother's hand. Together they walked toward the store.

When they got inside the store, Sandra

looked around. It was almost Christmastime. On the wall were some pictures of Santa Claus that children had colored. There were brightly colored boxes of cookies on the shelves.

"Come, Sandra," Mother said, leading Sandra toward the back of the store where the tools were.

While Mother was looking at the screwdrivers, Sandra stepped to the end of the aisle. Her eyes opened wide in surprise. A big Santa Claus was sitting in a chair nearby.

Sandra stared at Santa Claus. Then she felt Mother's hand on her shoulder. "Come, Sandra," Mother said.

"Mother," Sandra began.

Mother smiled down at Sandra. "You have some questions, don't you?" she asked. "Wait till we get to the car; then we will talk about them."

Finally Mother was done shopping, and they headed for the car.

"Mother," Sandra asked as Mother backed the car out of the parking space, "was that Santa Claus real? You said there isn't any Santa Claus."

"He was dressed up the way people say Santa Claus looks," Mother explained. "You see, Sandra, many fathers and mothers teach their children about Santa Claus. Grownups dress up as Santa Claus, and they ask the children what they want for Christmas. They say that Santa Claus brings presents to good little children at Christmastime. But really it is the fathers and mothers and other grownups who give the gifts. There is no real Santa Claus at all."

"They are telling a lie, aren't they?" Sandra asked, wide-eyed.

"Yes, they are," Mother answered. "And the Bible tells us, 'Lie not one to another.' That is the reason why Father and I have not told you children this made-up story about Santa Claus. We want to obey the Bible, and we want to teach you to obey too.

"When little children are taught about Santa Claus, they think more about him than about Jesus. They love him instead of Jesus. Anything that we love more than Jesus is like an idol, and we know that God does not want us to have idols.

"God is not pleased when parents teach their children to be good so that Santa Claus will bring them gifts. God wants parents to teach their children to love and honor Him."

"But why do the children believe in Santa Claus if he is a lie?" asked Sandra.

"Those children believe their fathers and mothers just like you believe what Father and I teach you," Mother explained. "God planned that children would trust their parents. God wants parents to teach their children to love and obey Him."

The next day Sandra was helping Mother bake cookies. She looked out the window and saw a blue car driving in the lane. "Oh, Mother, Mrs. Davis is here!" Sandra exclaimed.

"She's probably coming for her eggs," Mother answered, wiping her hands on her apron. "I'll go down to the basement to get them. You may invite her in."

Mrs. Davis came up the walk, and Sandra opened the door.

"Mother went to get your eggs," Sandra explained as Mrs. Davis stepped inside.

"Okay," Mrs. Davis answered. She looked over at the counter. "It smells good in here. Are you baking Christmas cookies?"

Sandra did not know what to say. "We're just baking cookies," she answered. "Mother said we need more for the schoolchildren's and Father's lunches."

"Did you go to see Santa Claus over at the mall this morning?" Mrs. Davis asked.

Sandra shook her head. Just then Mother came up the stairs with the eggs.

"Hello, Mrs. Andrews," Mrs. Davis said to Mother.

"Hello," Mother returned as she set the eggs on the table. "You wanted five dozen, right?"

"That's right," Mrs. Davis answered. "My two sisters are coming tomorrow, and we want to bake Christmas cookies. Is that what you're doing this morning?"

"We don't bake cookies especially for Christmas," Mother explained. "The children have vacation from school, and we do things together as a family then. Sometimes we go to visit friends on Christmas Day."

"Don't you even take your children to see Santa Claus?" Mrs. Davis asked.

Mother shook her head. "The Bible teaches that we should be truthful, and teaching children that there is a Santa Claus certainly isn't doing that.

"We teach our children that God sent His Son Jesus as a baby in a manger. We also teach them that He grew up and that He is their very best friend. Children are much happier when

they are told only the truth."

Mrs. Davis shrugged. She reached into her purse and pulled out her wallet. After paying for her eggs, she soon left.

"Mother, does Mrs. Davis believe in Santa Claus?" Sandra asked as she watched Mrs. Davis drive out the lane.

"Mrs. Davis knows that there is no Santa Claus," Mother answered, "but she still thinks that it's all right to teach children about him. She told her children about Santa Claus when they were little, and then when they were bigger, she had to tell them there is no Santa Claus after all."

Sandra's eyes grew big. "I wouldn't like that," she said. "Then they knew that their mother told a lie."

"Yes," Mother answered sadly. "God wants parents to be good examples to their children."

"I'm glad you and Father are good examples," Sandra said soberly. "I'm going to thank God for a father and mother who obey God and teach us true things."

"That is good," Mother said. "Thanking God for our blessings is another way to honor Him. Parents can only be good examples if they obey God and His Word. That is what Father and I want to do, and we want to teach you children to obey too."

"I want to obey God all the time," Sandra said as she watched Mother take a pan of cookies from the oven.

38.

A Good Listener

William drove his toy tractor back and forth on the rug, which he was using for his field. He was pretending to plant corn.

"William, I want you to pick up your toys now, and then vacuum the floor," Mother said.

William drove his tractor around the field several more times. He was thinking so much about planting corn that he almost forgot what Mother had said.

"William," Mother repeated.

"What, Mother?" William asked, looking up from his play.

"Pick up your toys now, and then vacuum this floor," Mother repeated. She sat down in the rocking chair with baby Verna.

William slowly put his tractor in the corner beside the toy box. He picked up the blocks that he had used to build his barn, and he put his cows in the toy box. Then he got out the sweeper and vacuumed the floor.

"Now will you read me a story while you feed Verna?" William asked.

"Yes, if you get me a book," Mother answered, smiling at William.

William went to the bookshelf. He already knew which book he wanted. He pulled *Daryl Borrows a Brother* from the shelf. He settled himself on the couch, and Mother opened the book and began to read.

Before long, Verna was asleep. Mother carried her to the bedroom, and then she went to the kitchen to make dinner. William sat on the couch and turned the pages, reading more of the story to himself.

"William," Mother called. "Please come and set the table."

William did not look up from his book. "This

story is so interesting. I don't want to set the table now," he thought.

"William!" Mother soon called again.

Slowly William closed his book. "What, Mother?"

"Come here, please," Mother said.

William walked to the kitchen. Mother was at the sink mixing flour and water to make gravy.

"William," Mother said, setting her little bowl on the counter, "did you really not hear what I said the first time?"

William hung his head.

"You heard me, didn't you?" Mother questioned.

Slowly William nodded.

"If you do not come the first time I call, that is not obeying me," Mother told him. "The next time I want you to come right away."

William nodded soberly as he went to wash his hands.

That afternoon William was busy coloring. "William, please go and get a diaper for Verna. Also bring her green dress that is in the top drawer of my dresser."

William was busy thinking about the rabbit he was coloring. He did not feel like going for

the things Mother wanted. But suddenly he remembered. Mother had said she wanted him to come right away when she called. He laid down his crayon and went to the bedroom. He picked up a diaper. "Now what else did Mother want?" He could not remember.

Slowly he walked out to Mother. He handed her the diaper.

"Where is Verna's dress?" Mother wondered.

"I—I forgot what else you said you wanted," William stammered.

"I want Verna's green dress that is in the top drawer of my dresser," Mother repeated.

William hurried to the bedroom and soon returned with the dress.

"William," Mother began, "you are getting into a bad habit. Sometimes when I ask you to do something, you ask, 'What, Mother?' Or you do not obey promptly, and then you forget what I said. When you really do not understand what I said, then you must ask. But you must learn to listen carefully the first time so that you do not need to ask 'What?' so often.

"The Bible tells us in James 1:19 that we should be 'swift to hear.' When we really want to obey, we will want to hear what we should do. It is very important for children to learn to be good listeners when they are young so that they will be ready to listen when God calls them."

William listened soberly. He knew that he had not really wanted to obey Mother.

"There will be times when you really do not understand what I say the first time," Mother said kindly. "But I want you to try very hard to be a good listener."

"I will try to be a good listener," William promised.

The next day William was playing in the sandbox when he heard something. He looked up and listened very carefully. Was Mother calling him? He was not sure.

"I'll go and see," he decided. He ran to the house.

"Mother, did you call me?" he asked breathlessly.

"No, I didn't, William," Mother said. She looked puzzled for a moment; then she smiled. "You must have heard me when I scolded Rover for lying in the flower bed. But, William, I am so glad you came when you thought I might have called you. I can tell that you are trying to learn to be a good listener.

"That reminds me, William, of a little boy in

the Bible who was a good listener," Mother said. "Do you know who that little boy was?"

William thought for a moment. "Was it Samuel?"

"That's right," Mother agreed. "Samuel lived with Eli the priest. One night he heard some-one calling him. What did he do?"

"He ran to Eli," William answered.

"That's right. This happened three times, and each time Samuel got up and went to Eli. Don't you think he could have gotten tired of obeying when Eli always said he hadn't called?"

William nodded. "He could have decided that he was just going to go to sleep instead of obeying."

"That's right. But he didn't. And because Samuel was an obedient boy, God was able to talk to him. God gave a message to Samuel. And when Samuel grew older, he was God's prophet. He helped the people of Israel to know what God wanted them to do."

"I want to be a good listener like Samuel," William decided.

"Good," Mother answered. "That is what we want you to do."

William ran outside to play again. He was

glad he had gone to see if Mother wanted him. He knew he had made Mother happy, and he was happy too.

"William!" Father called a little later from the shop.

William looked over toward the shop door.

"Could you please tell Mother that I will be fifteen minutes later for dinner?" Father called.

William was not sure what Father had said. "What shall I do?" he asked himself. "Mother doesn't want me to ask 'What?' so many times. I was trying to be a good listener today, but I didn't hear what Father said." He thought for a moment. "I guess I'll ask Mother about it. I do want to obey Father."

He ran to the house. "Mother—" He stopped, not knowing what to say.

"Yes, dear?" Mother turned from the counter and looked at his distressed face.

"I—I was trying to be a good listener, but—but—"

"But what?" Mother asked kindly.

"Father called to me and told me to tell you something, but I don't know what he said." William looked up into Mother's face.

"That is all right," Mother said kindly. "I know you were trying to be a good listener. You

338

came promptly when you thought I called you. This is one of those times when you didn't hear, even if you were trying. Run out and ask Father what he said."

Mother put her hand on William's shoulder. "Sometimes I have to ask another person to repeat what he said too. The most important thing is that you really want to obey, and I know you did."

William hurried out to the shop. "Father," he panted, "what did you want me to tell Mother? I tried to be a good listener, like Mother said, but I didn't hear you."

Father smiled. "I want you to tell Mother that I will be fifteen minutes later for dinner."

"You will be fifteen minutes later for dinner," William repeated. "Okay, Father, I will tell her that."

"I am happy that you are trying to be a good listener, son," Father said. "It is good to ask questions when we do not understand something, but first we must make sure that we are listening well. Grownups who have learned to listen well are the ones that God can use in His work."

William smiled up at Father. "Being a good listener makes me happy too," he said.

"That is because it is God's way," Father said. "God's way is always the right way, and it is the happy way."

Happily William skipped to the house to give Father's message to Mother. He was glad that he had tried to be a good listener, and he was glad that Father and Mother had understood that he really did try. He wanted to keep on trying to be a very good listener.

Just the Right Size

"Ride-a-ride-a-horsie!" Big sister Phyllis sat on the couch in the living room. She gently bounced baby Joan on her knees. Joan giggled happily.

"Do that to me!" begged four-year-old Annie. "Please, Phyllis."

"You're too heavy, Annie," Phyllis explained. "You could sit on my knee, and I could bounce you a few times, but I would get tired very quickly. Joan is a baby, but you are a big girl. You are too big for me to bounce on my knee.

I would get too tired and you might fall."

"No, I'm not," Annie disagreed. "Please?"

"No, Annie," Mother said firmly. "You heard what Phyllis said. You are too heavy for Phyllis to bounce on her knee."

Annie put her thumb in her mouth and curled up in the corner of the couch. A pout came over her face.

"Annie, come with me," Mother said. She helped Annie off the couch and led her to the bedroom.

Annie started to cry. "I'll be good, Mother. Please don't spank me."

Mother closed the bedroom door. "I think you need to be punished to help you remember not to pout when Mother tells you something," Mother said kindly but firmly. "You must obey Mother, and you must learn to do it sweetly." Mother opened the dresser drawer and took out the paddle.

After the spanking, Mother took Annie on her lap. Annie put her thumb in her mouth and snuggled up to Mother. Mother pulled Annie's thumb out of her mouth. "Remember, Annie, Mother doesn't want you to suck your thumb. You are getting to be a big girl."

Mother and Annie went out to the living

room together. Baby Joan was lying on the floor, sucking her thumb.

"No, no, Joan, you mustn't suck your thumb!" Annie pulled Joan's thumb out of her mouth. Joan started to cry.

"Annie," Mother said, "leave Joan alone."

"But, Mother, Joan was sucking her thumb," Annie said. "You don't let me suck my thumb."

"You are bigger than Joan," Mother explained patiently. "When Joan gets bigger, she must learn not to suck her thumb too."

Slowly Annie walked out to the kitchen. Phyllis was peeling apples to make a salad.

"May I help?" Annie asked eagerly.

"No, dear," Phyllis answered. "You are too little to peel apples. You might cut yourself. But you may stand on a chair and watch me."

"Mother," Annie cried, "why am I too big *and* too little? You said I am a big girl. But Phyllis won't let me peel apples."

Mother sat down and took Annie on her lap. "How old are you, Annie?" she asked.

"I'm four." Annie held up four fingers.

"That's right," Mother agreed. "And how old is Mervin?"

"He's seven." Annie held up seven fingers. "He showed me."

"Good," Mother answered. "Now, Mervin is a big boy. He can feed the calves for Father, and he takes good care of his rabbits. When Father fixes the fence, Mervin can help by giving him the right tools. And Mervin is learning to mow the lawn. All those things help Father and me very much. But can Mervin milk the cows all by himself like Father does?"

"No." Annie shook her head.

"Can Mervin drive the big tractor to bale hay?" Mother asked next.

"No, he is too little." Annie laughed.

"You are a big girl too, Annie," Mother explained. "You help Mother by drying the dishes. You fold the washcloths and the hankies. You pick up the toys. You run errands for me, like bringing a diaper when I need to change Joan."

Annie nodded. She liked to be Mother's helper.

"But some things you cannot do yet," Mother went on. "When Phyllis was four years old, she did not peel apples either. But she got bigger, and now she can peel apples and do many other jobs that are too big for a four-year-old. You are getting bigger too, and you are learning to do more and more things."

Mother smiled at Annie and said, "God has a special plan for families. He has work for mothers to do, and He has work for fathers to do. He has work for big children and work for little children. We are happy when we do the work God has planned for us."

"How can I know the work that God has planned for me?" Annie asked, puzzled.

"When you obey Mother and Father, you are doing what God planned for you," Mother explained. "The Bible says, 'Keep thy father's commandment, and forsake not the law of thy mother.' A commandment and a law mean the things that you are told to do. Keeping the commandment means being obedient. That is God's plan for children."

Mother stood up and set Annie on the floor. "Right now I need a helper to run to the garden and get two big red tomatoes for dinner. Who do you think is just the right size for that job?"

"Me!" Annie shouted eagerly.

"That's right," Mother answered with a smile. "Pick them carefully, like I showed you yesterday. And make sure they are red all over."

"I will, Mother." Annie hurried outside through the fresh green grass to the garden. Soon she returned with two big red tomatoes.

"Thank you, Annie," Mother said. "These look very good."

"I'm just the right size that God made me, right, Mother?" Annie asked.

"Right!" Mother gave Annie a big hug. "Just the right size to be Mother's special little helper."

"I'm glad," Annie said happily. "I like to be a helper."